JEANNE ELLINGTON

VOYAGE
TO
ROMANCE

A Prelude to Happiness

WestBow
PRESS
A DIVISION OF THOMAS NELSON

WestBow Press books may be ordered through booksellers or by contacting:

WestBow Press
A Division of Thomas Nelson
1663 Liberty Drive
Bloomington, IN 47403
www.westbowpress.com
1-(866) 928-1240

Because of the dynamic nature of the Internet, any web addresses or links contained in this book may have changed since publication and may no longer be valid. The views expressed in this work are solely those of the author and do not necessarily reflect the views of the publisher, and the publisher hereby disclaims any responsibility for them.

Any people depicted in stock imagery provided by Thinkstock are models, and such images are being used for illustrative purposes only.

Certain stock imagery © Thinkstock.

ISBN: 978-1-4497-3248-6 (hc)
ISBN: 978-1-4497-3247-9 (sc)
ISBN: 978-1-4497-3246-2 (e)

Library of Congress Control Number: 2011962534

Printed in the United States of America

WestBow Press rev. date: 01/18/2012

ACKNOWLEDGMENT

To Tom
My Forever Love

For his faithful help and encouragement in this and my
other computer projects, without which I couldn't have
accomplished them.

CAST OF CHARACTERS

Renee Darcel--(Pronounced Renay) Five feet seven, with light brown hair worn in a pony tail; blue-gray eyes, slender and well built. Works as a waitress since high school. Very outgoing and friendly. Age 19.

Rob Farnsworth--Tall, dark and handsome Army Captain, stationed in Paris, France for two years. Hails from Dallas, Texas. College Degree in Accounting. Age 24.

Ria Darcel--Five feet six, hazel eyes, dark brown hair, worn mostly up. Very slender, but well proportioned. Smart dresser; intelligent. Works as Secretary. Age 22.

Anne Darcel--Mother of Ria and Renee. Registered Nurse. Born in America but lived in France since childhood. Widowed three years. Very attractive. Age 56.

Jim Farnsworth--Married to Janet. Father of Rob and Eileen. Retired Corporate Lawyer. Handsome, very family oriented. Age 62.

Janet Farnsworth--Married to Jim. Mother of Rob and Eileen. Retired Controller of large Corporation. Attractive, very pleasant. Age 60.

Eileen (Farnsworth) Clark--Married to Keith Clark. Daughter of Jim and Janet, sister to Rob. Currently manager of Human Resources in small firm in Dallas.

Keith Clark--Married to Eileen. Currently a Civil Engineer with major oil company.

Craig Thornton--Minister, Church of Christ in Dallas.

Lynn Thornton--Wife of Craig

Maude Baldwin--Cook for Farnsworth family for many years.

Lois McCall--Housekeeper for Rob.

Pierre Darnell Interior Designer, Co-owner of large drapery and design company. Long-time boyfriend of Ria Darcel. Age 25.

Nicole (Darnell)Roget--Pierre's sister.

David Wallace--Young Lieutenant, friend of Rob's; also stationed in France.

Brandon Scott--Retired newspaper owner from Missouri. Gray hair, blue eyes, about five feet eleven. Widower of three years. Long-time friend of Gordon and Meg Brown. Age 60.

Gordon Brown--Retired Corporate Lawyer. Long-time friend of Brandon Scott from New York City. Husband of Meg.

Meg Brown--Retired High School English Teacher. Wife of Gordon. They have two daughters, both single, age 21 and 23.

Betty Marshall--Widow on cruise from Detroit, Michigan, traveling alone who met up with Renee and Anne on trip to New York. Became friend of Anne and later, Brandon and Browns.

Ron's Accounting Staff:
Accountants:
George White (wife--Marge)
Mike Sanders (wife Beth)
Karen Busby--single

Administrative Assistant:
Katie Masters

It was a foggy, gray day the "*Voyager*" arrived in New York, but to Renee, it was a shining mist in the air almost obscuring the lights from New York harbor, within shouting distance now.

There it was, the beautiful Statue of Liberty Rob had always spoken of so often. Rob, six feet four inches of tall, dark handsomeness and of whom Renee had thought of continually since the letter came that day.

Oh yes--the letter, Renee thought, and her heart started beating furiously and small beads of sweat appeared on her forehead.

Suddenly, with a surge of excitement, it occurred to her that only a few days ago, she had given up all hope that she would ever be Rob's chosen one. The letter he had written to her Mother was just a piece of paper but it had words on it that had changed her whole life.

She had, in retrospect, loved Rob almost the first time she had met him. She had been working at a small café in Paris when a tall, handsome American came in. She had gone to his table to take his order and he kept looking at the menu and he seemed reluctant to speak.

So in her very effective English, she asked what he'd like to order. He said "thank goodness, you can speak English. I must confess I don't speak French, so I don't know how to order". Renee was very glad to help and they started having a nice conversation. She loved his smile, his voice, and his smell, which was a mixture of shaving lotion and mint mouthwash.

After that, Rob came in often and always sat in the area where Renee was serving. She looked forward to his coming and could hardly wait to see his smile, disarming as it was to her.

There were times she could hardly speak when she first saw him. Her heart would begin to beat rapidly and her breathing shallow. If he happened to touch her accidentally with his arm when she was serving him, she felt 'goose bumps' all over. She would hurry home from work and spend a little time alone in her room just thinking about what had gone on while he was there. She thought, "so this is the way it feels to be in love."

Rob's visits to the café became regular and she looked forward to seeing him. In fact, she was very disappointed when he failed to come in. He and Renee became great friends. He teased her and they laughed together and when he asked how old she was and she said 19, he told her he hoped he'd be around when she grew up. She was secretly disappointed because she realized that he thought of her as a little girl.

Renee decided to ask her mother's permission to bring him home to dinner and she was pleased to have him come. Renee had talked so much about him, Anne felt she already knew him.

However, there was one thing that made her a little reluctant to invite him over--Renee secretly worried about introducing him to her older sister, Ria, who was a very pretty girl and "just the right age" for Rob. Renee knew she'd never feel the same way about anyone as she did Rob. She felt that being only 19 wasn't too far away from 24, Rob's age. Why did it have to make such a difference how old people were?

When Rob came over, he was very gracious to both her mother and to Ria. They seemed to be getting very well acquainted. She realized he was really getting into a long conversation with Ria and they were asking each other all sorts of questions. In fact, she could see they were becoming involved. Too much so! The girls had always been close and never jealous of each other. So this was a new feeling for her to actually be feeling jealous of her own sister!

Rob continued to come into the café to see Renee and he told her she had done him a great favor in bringing him to her house. He was attracted to Ria and had decided to ask her out. Renee could tell that he considered her a good friend, but he had no idea that she had strong romantic feelings about him. She felt like her heart would break!

For some time, Ria had been fairly serious with a young Frenchman who was in Interior Design. Ria liked being in the company of important people and loved dressing up and going to exciting places. However, Pierre's work was taking more and more of his time and wasn't allowing much time for Ria. Consequently, she had just recently decided to break up with him and to "play the field."

Rob came at just the right time for Ria to try someone "new". When he found that she was uninvolved, he asked her out several weeks in a row. Before long, it appeared to be getting serious between them. In fact, they were dating each other exclusively. Ria began to say she wouldn't be surprised if they started to talk about marriage. Renee's heart was breaking, but she couldn't bring herself to tell anyone about it, especially Ria.

Rob's visits to the café were still very friendly, but it felt different to Renee. Then he started to bring Ria there too and when they would leave, he would very teasingly kiss her on the cheek and call her his sweet little girl. This was very painful for her. After work, she would go to her room and cry her heart out. She mentally locked her heart and threw away the key for she no longer had any hope for herself and Rob.

Rob and Ria would ask her to go to the movies with them occasionally and Rob would always sit between them. He would reach over and hold Renee's hand on one side while holding Ria's on the other. Ria didn't mind as she thought he was in love with her and she was pleased that they were such good friends. Rob mentioned often that they looked a lot alike. In fact, he said Ria looked like a "grown up" version of Renee. This didn't make Renee too happy as it made her further realize that Rob thought she was too young for him.

Renee, Ria and their mother were a very close-knit family and had always had a very good relationship. They had no other relatives close by. Their father had been killed in an accident three years ago and their mother earned their living as a nurse. Ria had a job as a secretary in a downtown firm. There wasn't enough money for Renee to go to college so she had gotten a job as a waitress in the small café where she and Rob met. With the turn of events between Rob and Ria, Renee felt and acted somewhat cool to Ria, who had no idea it concerned her and ignored it.

Ria told Renee that she thought she loved Rob and mentioned that she thought he was so handsome. She also became very excited when she talked of going to the United States to live. She said, "you could come over and visit in America, which is something you have always said you wanted to do. Wouldn't that be great?" Renee said "I guess so." but Ria had no idea how her romance with Rob was affecting Renee. She was very pleased that her family liked Rob so much.

So far, Renee had been able to conceal her feelings about Rob from Ria, but her Mother noticed that she had lost her appetite and began to look very pale. She asked her what was wrong and Renee would just shrug her shoulders and say she was okay. She began to ask herself what she could do to forget him. Then she had a plan. She would ask to take extra shifts and then she wouldn't be at home when he came to see Ria. She would also make some extra money and that way, she might be able to go to America on her own someday.

She did this for several weeks and found herself getting so tired she had to go back to only one shift. She turned down invitations from her girlfriends as well as boys who asked her out. She became very depressed and showed no interest in going anywhere or doing anything. Her Mother became very worried about her and tried to encourage her to do things with her friends, but she wasn't at all open to her suggestions.

One day when Rob came over, he said "Hey Sweets, would you consider double dating with me and Ria? I have a young friend who is very homesick and he could surely use some cheering up." Rob thought to himself that Renee could use some, too. He couldn't understand what was wrong with her. She had always had such a sunny disposition and was fun to be around, but lately, she had seemed like a different person. "I told him you were a real sweetheart and pretty too and he was very interested. How about it, will you go?" At first, Renee didn't want to but then she thought she should at least try to get over it due to the fact that Ria and Rob were a couple serious about each other and there was nothing she could or would do about that. So she agreed to go.

Rob's friend, David, was a slender, young man about 5 ft 9 inches tall, blonde and blue-eyed. The direct opposite of Rob, Renee thought in her mind. David had a nice smile and was very polite. He was also very shy and didn't seem to know how to carry on a conversation. Renee kept asking him questions to try to get acquainted with him but it seemed next to impossible. He would answer questions with a one or two-syllable word and never elaborate on the topic of conversation at all. Needless to say, Renee felt it was a very boring date. She vowed she would not see him again.

Several times within the next few weeks, Rob would ask if she would see David again on a double date and she refused, saying she would select her own dates. Secretly, she just didn't think she could stand to see Rob and Ria together any more than necessary.

She continued to be sad and lonely because she just was not interested in anyone else. One day, her Mother came to her room to have a serious talk with her and find out just what her problems were and she found her crying.

Her Mother took her in her arms and she confessed her feelings for Rob. Her mother told her she was so sorry but that she must understand that love had to be between two people who felt the same way to make it work. She said it was nice that she thought so highly of Rob but that she must face the facts and go on with her life. Although Renee understood this, it did not help her feelings for Rob at all.

By the time six months had passed, Rob and Ria were dating twice a week. When he came to town on a work day on business, however, he would still drop into Le Café Rouge and chat with Renee, while having a cup of coffee. He would tell her all about America and Texas. He told her he was anxious to go back and start his Accounting business in Dallas. He also told her he would really like for her and her mother to come over for a visit as they had been so hospitable to him, he wanted to repay them in some way.

Then the "blow" came. It was a happy one for Rob because it meant he was going home. His auditing assignment had ended, he said, and now he was going back home to Texas. He was anxious to see his family and get his business office set up with money he had saved. He had his accounting degree already and was all set to take his CPA exam when he got home. He started making plans to go home and told them all he would write. He asked Renee to write to him too.

Ria was surprised and a little hurt that he didn't make a definite commitment to marry her. However, she realized they had not known each other very long even though she thought they loved each other. And too, Rob had always told her that he needed to get his business started before he could even think about marriage to anyone.

Renee was heartbroken at the thought of never seeing Rob again but she did promise to write as he asked her to do. He gave her a big hug and kiss on the cheek when he said goodbye.

After Rob had gone home, he had been writing to Renee and Ria separately. He told Rene that he had such pleasant memories of his time there that he was actually "homesick" for them and their mother. He said he had passed his CPA exam, and set up his new office. He had also bought a new car.

He asked Ria in a letter if she would like to come over to see him. He said he felt that before they could even think of making a permanent commitment, they needed to see each other again and see how they felt about each other after being apart. In addition, he wanted her and his family to meet and for her to see how she liked Texas and America.

Ria told him she was excited about coming over to meet his family and wanted to know how long it would be before she could come over. He told her he would apply for the visa but he didn't know how long it would take.

7

After several weeks, the request for the immigration visa for Ria to go to America had still not come through and Ria was getting very impatient.

In the meantime, Pierre had come back on the scene and kept begging her to go out again and she decided to do so. This disturbed Ria's mother and Renee greatly, because they felt she was not being honest with Rob. In addition, Ria asked Renee not to mention it to him. She said that she wouldn't have anyway as she would do nothing to hurt her sister but she told her that she didn't think it was right. Secretly, she didn't care except that she felt it wasn't fair to Rob.

In the meantime, Rob felt that things were not right between him and Ria, but he couldn't quite put his finger on the problem. By her letters, which became more infrequent as time went on, he knew she was becoming impatient and less interested as her letters had all but stopped.

However, he was still receiving regular letters from Renee and it was the one bright spot in his life when he got a letter from her. He was constantly reminded of the good times he had enjoyed in their home.

In her last letter, Renee included a picture of herself and Ria and when he saw Renee's picture, it dawned on him like a bolt out of the blue--<u>Renee</u> was the one he had been envisioning all the time he was feeling lonesome for them!! Could it be possible that she was the one he loved all the time? His answer from his heart said "yes!"

Now he was in a fine mess! How in the world could he break up with one sister and propose to the other? Then he thought to himself that his only solution would be to talk it over with their mother. Mrs. Darcel was a very sweet and understanding person and she would tell him honestly whether he could make this happen or not. So he decided to write her a letter.

May 2, 2011
Dallas, Texas

My dear Mrs. Darcel:

I know you are going to be surprised at getting a letter from me instead of a greeting in the girls' letters, but I have a matter of great importance to discuss with you and I will abide by your advice.

I have known for some time that things between me and Ria have not been the way I had thought they would be. I am more and more convinced that we are not going to make each other happy and that is not the way a marriage should be. In fact, unknown to her, I have several soldier friends who are still in the area over there who see her dating others on a regular basis. So I don't feel it would be any surprise to her or would really matter to her if I broke it off with her. I certainly would not want to hurt her, but I feel this is what I have to do. What do you think?

That is only one problem. My other problem is this and it is the most important decision of my life. I have realized more and more that the person I miss the most in the world is Renee and I know it is really her that I love and want to ask to be my wife. Deep down, I feel Renee loves me too. We are very good friends first, but I know there has always been real affection there too. I guess the old saying "absence makes the heart grow fonder" must be true.

Now what do you think about all this? Is it hopeless? Am I a terrible person? Please write to me as soon as possible. I will await your answer and, of course, your permission, most anxiously.

With kindest regards
Rob

When Anne finished reading the letter, she decided she'd better have a cup of tea before making any decisions. She knew for sure about one, though. Renee was going to be completely thrilled over the whole thing as she had been carrying Rob in her heart ever since he first met him.

Now as far as Ria was concerned, how could she care a whole lot with the way she'd been seeing other people and neglecting to write to Rob? Frankly, she'd been thinking of sitting her down and insisting that she write to him or even writing to Rob and breaking it off herself, because Ria seemed to have quit caring about him. That had made Anne very unhappy for she really cared about Rob and had looked forward to having him in their family. Lately, however, she had given up hope.

Now, it looked as if it could become a reality, after all. She could hardly wait to tell Renee the news and she planned to tell her right away. However, she had to make her plan first, on how to approach it.

After she had a good hot cup of tea, she decided that she would talk to each girl separately and let them read Rob's letter as it would be better coming straight from him. She was sure Rob was right about it not bothering Ria very much, if at all. But then, you never know about things like that. It could be a little ticklish.

She had the day off from the hospital, so she'd fixed a special meal for the girls that night. When they got home, she said she wanted to have a talk with each of them separately sometime after dinner. Ria said she had a date so her mother said they'd talk when she came home. She tried to get her mother to give her a hint what it was about, but she said she'd have to wait. Renee helped her mother do the dishes after dinner and when Ria left, they sat down to talk.

Her mother told her it had to do with Rob and that she wanted her to read his letter and hold any comment until she was completely through with it. As she opened the letter and started to read, she had a very confused look on her face.

Of course, Anne was watching every move that Renee made and as she got further down into the letter, she saw her face turn red, saw her swallow hard and then start to cry. With tears streaming down her face, she said "Oh Mama, my dream is really coming true. My prayers are answered. I didn't see how it could possibly come about, but I kept believing that somehow, some way it would and now it has! When can I talk to Rob?" "Oh Mama, I am so happy."

Her Mother took her in her arms and told her she was so glad for her and that it had worked out because it was right for her. "I promised to write back to Rob, but he said he would telephone you before that. It will probably be tomorrow. I know that you both need that."

"I know that I'll never be able to sleep a wink--I don't even have to sleep to dream now!" said Renee and she hugged her Mother goodnight.

Soon after Renee had gone to bed, Ria came in with an animated look on her face and said. "Oh Mama, you will never guess what happened tonight. I know that you know Pierre and I have been seeing each other again. Well, tonight, he said he had a surprise for me.

So we went out to a very romantic dinner with candles and everything and he asked me to marry him. He gave me this beautiful ring when I said yes. Isn't it just gorgeous?

I never really got over Pierre, I am sure you already know, and when Rob came along so nice and available, it helped me take my mind off Pierre temporarily. And now that I think of it, he never had actually told me he was in love with me. I know he liked me a lot and we enjoyed going out together but I also got to thinking that even if I went over there to see him, what if it didn't work out and in my heart, I guess I didn't even want it to as the first chance I got, I started seeing Pierre again.

Her Mother said, "Well, this is a surprise. I knew you had been seeing other people but did not know it had been exclusively Pierre or that you were really serious about him. I am very pleased that you are happy, darling, and your ring is gorgeous but I have a question--what had you planned to do about Rob? When you commit yourself to someone, you should not go out with others unless you first break it off with them. Don't you realize that was not fair?"

"Well, it isn't as if we were engaged exactly, although we were not seeing anyone else and I suppose it was understood at least by Rob that we would still not see others. I meant to write to him and tell him I had gone back to seeing Pierre, but I just didn't know quite how to do it." "What was it that you wanted to talk to me about?"

Well, what I have to tell you is that I have a letter from Rob that I want you to read. Please read it completely before you make any comment. Okay?"

Ria took the letter and began to read. Her face turned pale and she began to shift in her chair as if she was uncomfortable. Then she read on and her eyes began to blink in surprise and when she finished the letter, she folded it and put it in the envelope. She then said, "Well, I guess my news just solved the whole problem, didn't it?"

"Well, it solves the problem in that you have fallen in love and that you will be happy and also, that Renee and Rob will be happy together at last. I can tell you now that your little sister has been in love with him since she first met him. Now that he has realized that it is she that he loves, I think it is wonderful. If that hadn't been the case, we could have had a real problem."

"But that isn't the end of it, Ria. I am going to answer Rob's letter, but I feel that you owe him an apology for not being up front and honest with him when you knew that it was Pierre you loved and not him. I realize it turned out all right but you should be aware that you could have been the one hurt if you still loved Rob and he had realized his love for Renee. I'd say that 'all's well that ends well' if you do that."

"I think you are right, Mama. Rob is a wonderful person and I have really been worrying that I would hurt him by breaking it off. I had absolutely no idea that Renee felt that way about him but I am glad that he has realized his love for her. He always seemed to have a real soft spot for her and had more to talk to her about than he ever did me. Why didn't she say something to me if she felt that way?"

"Now you know that she would not do a thing like that if she thought you loved each other and she did think that."

"Well, I want to run upstairs and talk to Renee right away. We have a lot to say to each other."

"I think you do. It seems that things haven't been quite right between you two for some time."

"I know it, Mama and it has been bothering me, but honestly, I had no idea why. I guess I should have asked her myself, but she probably wouldn't have told me."

Renee and Ria talked and hugged and cried and laughed most of the night they were so excited. They had always been very close and shared secrets with each other but lately, they had seemed to drift apart because each was carrying a secret she just couldn't share. Now things were right between them again.

Next day, Anne Darcel sat down and wrote her letter to Rob.

May 5, 2011
Paris, France

Dear Rob:

I was surprised to receive your letter, but I must say I was not at part of its content. I am flattered that you trust my judgment. However, I don't think you really have a problem at all now! Read on. I have no need to comment on your second problem for the following reasons.

I know that Renee has been in love with you from the day she met you. She was heartbroken when you started dating Ria steadily.

I let each of them read your letter. Renee says her prayers have been answered and her dreams have come true to know that you love her the same way she loves you. I am delighted that I still have a chance to have you as a son-in-law!

Ria was not surprised that you felt you were not right for each other. When she came in last night, she had some news that confirmed that. She has gone back to Pierre and they got engaged just last night! She says she is going to write you a letter as she is sorry for not being up front with you. She just had really not gotten over Pierre when she met you, I guess.

I am sending this to you in Special Delivery Overnight Mail so that as soon as you get it, you can call Renee. I am not sure of the time difference there, but I am sure that you are.

Thank you, my dear for sharing this with me. It has made me very happy because we all love you and are so glad you want to be part of our family.

My Best to You Always
Anne

Paris, France
May 7, 2011

Dear Rob:

I want to tell you that I was relieved when Mama let me read your letter. For weeks, I have been worrying about how to tell you that I am still in love with Pierre. I really love you as a person, Rob, and I was very flattered that you thought you you cared enough about me to have me come over to see you again and to meet your family.

If there had been no "waiting time" for the Immigration Visa, and I could have accompanied you home to Texas, I probably would have. But thank the Good Lord, that didn't happen, because it would have been wrong for both of us, since we each one are in love with another!

Pierre asked me to marry him last night and I accepted. I am sure it is the right thing for me. I am so glad that you also "woke up" to the fact that you are in love with my little sister. As you know, she is a wonderful person and to think she kept her feelings for you inside her all of this time. I could not have done it, I don't think, but she has a very strong sense of right and wrong which is something I need to learn from her. Anyway, Rob, I am truly delighted you will be in our family. Maybe you and I can learn to be friends now. I think that was part of what was wrong in our relationship. We weren't friends first and I think that is very important. I hope you and Pierre will like each other. He is a very nice man too.

I do apologize for my insensitivity but let's face it, if I had been as nice as my sister, you might have just had to settle for me! Just kidding! Take care of yourself. I hope we see you again before too long.

Sincerely, Ria

Rob was very surprised and excited to get an overnight special delivery from Anne. He whooped for joy as he read her first few lines as it told him exactly what he longed to know--that Renee loved him the way he loved her.

As he finished the letter, he was relieved to know that there was no problem with Ria either and was glad she would be marrying Pierre. He really had caught her on the rebound as she had just broken up with Pierre when they met and started dating.

"Well, I have two things to do. I have to contact Immigration and see if I can change the name on the VISA and somehow expedite the processing of it. Then he realized this action was really premature until he actually talked to Renee.

So he checked the time and placed a call. Renee had been anxiously awaiting this important phone call, so she answered promptly, with the statement, "Hello Rob. This is Renee."

"Hello my darling Renee. How wonderful that feels to actually say that to you when I have been thinking of it for days now. Before you say anything, let me tell you that I have been dreaming of you day and night for the past two weeks. Ever since I got the picture you sent, I have been on pins and needles to get this whole thing straightened out."

Renee started to breathe deeply and couldn't help it when she began to cry. "I am so happy Rob."

"Renee, sweetheart, please don't cry. I want you to know that you are first in my heart and I always want you to feel that way. It is as if I was asleep and had an amazing awakening to something that was there all the time. Does that make any sense at all? I love you with all my heart and want you to be my wife. Now that I have had my say, it is your turn, what do you have to say to me?"

"Oh Rob, I am so happy at all you said to me. I love you with all of my heart too and I always have. I just prayed that somehow, some way it would work out that you would love me too. I have always been very happy that we were such good friends, but it just wasn't enough."

"I would like more than anything to be your wife and live with you in Texas or any place you say. This is just the very best thing that has ever happened to me. Do you have any idea when we might see each other?"

"I have contacted the Immigration Office and they assure me that it will be no problem for me to change the name on the visa application. I will need you to fill out a form I will send to you immediately and will send you a prepaid envelope to return it in overnight mail. You will need to include a certified copy of your birth certificate."

"Do you think it would be possible for me to come and visit and meet your family while we are waiting for the permanent visa?"

"I don't know, Sweets, but I will certainly check into it. That is a great idea. We may find a way to get married when you come. How about asking your Mother if she would like to do that too, and you could come together. She probably has some vacation time coming and I will pay for both of you to come if it can be worked out. See if she can possibly get leave for a month so she can be here for our wedding."

"Okay, I will ask her. I really think she can and will."

"Bye for now, my Sweets--remember I love you very much."

"Bye to you too, Rob and I love you too--jai tres vous aimez."

When she received the envelope from Rob, she immediately wrote a sweet follow-up note, enclosed the necessary papers, and sent it off to him.

She received a letter from him acknowledging hers very promptly.

Dallas, Texas
May 12, 2011

My darling Renee:

I received your letter along with the papers I needed. Thank you for sending them so promptly. I enjoyed talking to you and can't wait to see and talk to you in person. I also can't wait to hold you in my arms and really kiss you properly. Do you realize that the only kisses I have ever given you have been on your forehead and your cheek? I guess you do realize that, but you will have to admit that for an "engaged" couple, it is unusual. We are going to make up for lost time when you come. I intend to smother you with kisses and hugs. I hope you want that, too!

I contacted the American Embassy here and found that if I just apply for a visitor's visa to get you over here, we can get married and the permanent one will be very easy to get when we prove we are married. I will apply for your Mom's visitor visa at the same time. I am really glad she can come too.

So, get your "planning hat" on and let me know as soon as possible when you and your Mom would like to sail over. I intend to get you on a nice ocean liner if possible so that you can enjoy the voyage over.

We will plan to spend at least a couple of nights in New York to let you rest a bit and, perhaps, take in a show if I can manage to get tickets, before we travel on to Dallas. Does that sound like something you would like to do?

When we get to Dallas, we will all go to my folks' home for a day or two as they insist that we do so to get acquainted. I have reservations for a hotel suite for you and your Mom when you feel you need to have some private time to get ready for our wedding. Of course, we will be spending a lot of time together planning it, but I also have a business to run so I will need to devote some time to it.

My Mom has phone numbers for practically everything we will need to put this whole scene on which will save us some time. She will do only what you want her to in order to help, so don't worry about her taking over because she is not like that. She is, in fact, a lot like your Mom and I think they will make a great team.

I just can't wait to see you, my darling. I love you all the way round the world and back!!

Rob

May 15, 2008
Dallas, Texas

My dearest Rob:

I just got your letter. What great news that we can go ahead and get married. I can't wait to see you either. It has been so long. To answer some of your questions: yes, it will be great to spend a few days with your parents to get to know each other. I will be looking forward to that. It is very thoughtful of them to invite us. Yes, I would love to see a Broadway show. It would be a great treat if you can get tickets. Don't worry if you can't. You are already going to a great deal of trouble and expense for us, and we appreciate it.

Ria is planning her wedding for May 29. Mama and I will be packed and ready to go anytime after that day -- even the next day. I think we'd arrive in NYC in 6 or 7 days.

As you know, Ria and Pierre have known each other a long time so they pretty well know what each other wants or thinks. They have already found an apartment and are busily furnishing it. Pierre is a professional interior designer so that is his "cup of tea." He is a part owner in a very nice furniture and drapery shop they are just having a small wedding with family and friends but she already has a gorgeous white dress. Incidentally, it also exactly fits me and she insists that it be my wedding dress too! What do you think about that?

I am sure our moms will be a great deal of help and it will be appreciated. Until I helped with Ria's wedding, I didn't realize all there is to do for even a small one.

I hope I have answered all of your questions. If not, ask me again in your next letter which I hope comes quickly. I just re-read your letter. Yes indeed, I will be happy to make up for lost time! In fact, I can hardly wait!

I Love you
With all of my heart
Renee

Renee, Ria, and their mother spent the next three days shopping until they were exhausted. "Well, that about does it for your trousseau, doesn't it Ria?"

"Yes, thank goodness."

"Then, I suggest we sit down and have some tea and discuss everything and look at our lists to see what all we need to do to get you and Pierre married."

"Well, we've selected the flowers, ordered the cake and food for the reception. Pierre and I have seen the minister, gotten our license. My dress, veil and shoes are ready; Renee's maid-of-honor dress is here along with her matching shoes. My going-away suit is ready. My new gown and peignoir set Renee gave me is ready."

Her Mom then said, "your new luggage is ready and we bought new lingerie and cosmetics so you should be ready to pack for your honeymoon anytime now. I can't think of anything else to be done can you?"

No, Mama, I can't and I really appreciate all you have both done to make it nice for us. We've invited only 50 people and those have all accepted our invitation. Your maid-of-honor dress looks so sweet on you, Renee, that you will be able to use it as a dress-up dress later."

"You are right. I like it very much and I wish you were going to wear it at my wedding. But you know what? I have a great idea. Since we are both the same size and I am taking your wedding dress, why don't you keep the maid-of-honor dress?"

"Well, maybe I will. I really could use another dressy outfit to take on our honeymoon. Since both dresses are made from the same pattern, I know I like it already. Thank you, Renee, I accept."

"You know, it is hard to believe that these next few days will be the last time we will be just <u>us</u> in our little family "Oh Mama, will you be terribly lonely?" Renee said as she reached over and gave her mother a big hug and a kiss on her cheek. "I feel badly, leaving you, even as happy as I am to be getting married to Rob."

"I don't want you to feel bad for a second. My whole aim in life has been to help you girls to have as nice a life as I could give you and to have you grow up and marry the man you love. That is what I am getting and I couldn't be happier.

Remember, I have a lot of friends and can have a lot more activities since I will be responsible for only myself. I have a career I love and wonderful people to work with. I can't ask for anything better than the way things are turning out."

"Well Renee, don't forget I will be close by to check on her. Don't you forget to write and tell us all about America and Texas in particular with specific emphasis on Dallas" Ria said, with a smile.

"Oh, I will definitely be in close touch with both of you. Don't worry about that. I hope I don't get homesick." "Well don't forget about phones, letters and e-mail to keep in touch."

"Oh, I definitely won't forget that."

"Well I am sure we will manage to see each other once in awhile. It probably won't be very often, due to the distance but we will be very interested in saving money for airfare between the two places, don't you think? I am sure that Rob will see to it that you get to come back to see us sometime as he says he has happy memories of his time here."

"I am sure of that, Mama."

"Oh, I know Pierre and I will, as we have already talked about the fact that we would like to take a vacation and come to see you and Rob. He says he has always wanted to see the United States."

"That would be great. Maybe we will have a house by the time you can come. Even if we don't, Rob says we will definitely get a two-bedroom apartment so that we have room for Mama and any other company we might have, which would certainly include you and Pierre."

'Well, let's call it a day and go to bed. Renee, you and I should plan to go shopping again tomorrow as I have to work the next two days after that. Get your list together like we had Ria do, so that we can we get as much done as possible."

"I already have my list made, Mama, and have marked off things I have done or purchased. Rob asked when we would be ready to leave and I told him we could leave the next day or so after Ria's wedding so he should be sending our tickets soon. I think it is awfully nice of him to arrange an Ocean Liner cruise for us instead of just an airline trip, don't you?"

"I certainly do. I also agree with you that we should have everything ready to go as soon as the kids get away on their honeymoon trip. I have already arranged for the leave of absence and Renee has said she will look in on the house when they return in a week to make sure everything is okay and that the sprinkler system is keeping our lawn healthy."

"Mama, Rob asked me to tell you that you will have no expenses except what you want to spend yourself on this trip. He said to tell you that you will have the hotel suite for as long as you are in Texas. Of course, the ocean trip is paid for and you will fly back home from Dallas."

"That is very sweet of Rob. He is a thoughtful and generous young man. But then, we already know that, don't we?"

"Yes, we certainly do. Well good night, Mama. See you in the morning."

During the next two weeks after writing to Rob, they talked on the phone and sent each other e-mail messages. Renee and her Mom bought her some new luggage, a new going-away outfit, some lingerie, and a new bathing suit, as Rob said she would need it in Dallas and that his folks had a nice pool that they could swim in.

The two weeks passed rather quickly and Ria and Pierre's wedding, while simple, was very beautiful. Pierre's sister, Nicole, was a bridesmaid, and his little three-year-old niece, Julie, was flower girl. Everything went off as planned and the happy couple went to Venice for their week-long honeymoon. Their apartment was ready to move into upon their return. Ria bade her Mom and Renee goodbye. They all hugged each other with just a couple of tearful moments.

Renee had received the tickets for their voyage several days ago and now the day for sailing was here at last. She was so excited, she was ready to burst.

The ocean liner named '*The Voyager*' was elegant, beautiful and huge! Renee and Anne made a point of walking through the entire ship on all five decks. They not only wanted to experience its beauty and luxury, but they knew it was great exercise. They played Shuffleboard, Bingo, and Gin Rummy. They read, wrote some letters and worked a large jigsaw puzzle. They also spent a great deal of time just eating. The food was absolutely wonderful and there were small eating places all over the ship--even hot dogs, hamburgers, French fries and ice cream for between meals. As if they needed more!

The voyage was more than they dreamed it could be. The night time entertainment was excellent as well. Although Renee could have been social with people her age, she preferred to spend it alone or just with her Mother as she was pretty occupied just dreaming of being with Rob.

Renee was very pleased to see how much her mother enjoyed herself. She met a number of people her age, some of whom were sailing together. Several times they asked her if she would play bridge with them as they needed someone to play. There was an extra man traveling with three couples and they recruited Anne and another single lady named Betty Marshall so they could have two tables. Anne and Betty became friends and they were soon regular players with the group. One of the couples was from New York City and they indicated they would like to see her while she was there, if possible.

Anne also became very aware of the single, clean-cut, graying gentleman with a beautiful resonant voice and noticed that more and more he arranged to be her partner. He asked her to lunch one day and they became very well acquainted. He told her his wife had died about three years before and that he had recently retired from being a newspaperman in Joplin, Missouri. His name was Brandon Scott and he had turned his newspaper over to his son, John. He seemed very interested in Anne and told her he had planned a trip to Europe in the near future and asked if he might come to see her when in France. She said she would like that.

She said to herself that she didn't realize she could have feelings for another man, but she had to admit, she did feel a spark of interest in him. The feeling was, obviously, mutual. She felt herself looking forward to spending time with him.

Brandon asked Anne how long she would be in New York and she told him only a couple of days before leaving for Dallas. She also told him Rob was trying to get tickets for a Broadway play. He then told her he was stopping for a visit with the New York City couple and asked if they might see each other. She said she didn't really know Rob's plans, but that they could wait and talk to him.

She asked Renee what she thought about it and Renee said, "I like Brandon Scott. He is a nice man. Why don't we talk to Rob when we see him and maybe he could join us for dinner and the Broadway Show?"

When Anne told Brandon this, he was delighted at the prospect. He told Gordon and Meg brown about it and they said, "Why don't we just have a foursome ourselves and let the newly-engaged couple have a night to themselves?

When Anne told Renee about that she laughed and said, "Its sounds like you are getting a rush, Mama. But I think it is great, if that is what you want to do. You will have plenty of time to see Rob and there isn't much time for you to see your new friend. So, go ahead and plan it. It doesn't really matter what Rob and I do, as long as we are together."

Her mother smiled and said, "I'm sure of that, my dear. And I am so happy for you that your dream is coming true."

At long last, the Captain announced that they would be arriving in New York about 10:00 am. Renee had arisen early and hadn't waited for the announcement to start packing and getting ready to see Rob.

She had been counting the days and hours again and she was almost breathless at the idea of seeing him in a different role this time. No longer was she the "little girl" who got a kiss on the forehead or cheek. Now she would soon be in Rob's arms, and get a real kiss. She was so ready to give him one too. She felt a shiver go down her back at just the thought.

She went out on deck and noticed that it was foggy. It seemed a little like London in a way. But then, she noticed lights in the distance and as they got closer in, she could see the outline of the statue welcoming them to New York.

It took about an hour before the ship came to a stop and they were told to congregate in certain places in preparation for departing the ship. It seemed to take forever but it was really only about another hour until their group was called. They, then, had to go through Customs which took another hour. It was now past noon and Renee was tired and hungry and anxious.

They stepped out on the pier and before she knew it, she was picked up bodily and given a crushing hug by Rob. He then set her down and gave her the most romantic kiss Renee could have even imagined. He said. "Sweets, I had forgotten just how beautiful you are. Your picture was so pretty but you are much prettier now. You grew up just like I thought you would. I am so glad you are here and I love you. I have missed your sweet smile. I can't wait until we get married."

"Oh Rob, I am so glad to see you. I thought we would never get here. The cruise was great and the ship so lovely but it would have been so much nicer if you had been with me too. I love you too so very much."

"Well, we will take a cruise together--don't you worry. I am looking forward to it. Rob looked over and saw Anne and said, "Oh hello Mrs. Darcel., I didn't mean to ignore you, but I am certain that you understand." and at that, he stepped over and embraced her.

Anne laughed and accepted the hug from Rob and said "I completely understand. I am so glad it worked out for you two as I think you deserve each other and I mean it in the nicest way."

"Thank you. Your opinion means a great deal to me and I think you already know that. I am so anxious for both of you to meet my family and they, you. We are going to go to their home for a few days when we first get to Dallas. They insist that it is the best way to really get to know each other. They have a very large home.

For now, we are going to a nice hotel here. We'll check in and freshen up and then go out to eat. I imagine you are starved. I know I am. How does that sound?"

"It sounds fantastic to me. I am famished." sighed Renee.

Sounds great to me too. I think I could go for a nap afterwards if you two don't mind. This kid had me up before dawn." said Anne, as she stifled a yawn.

"That would be fine. Whatever you want to do is okay by me. How about you, Sweets--do you need a nap?"

"No, I don't. I want to walk around and see a bit of New York and just be with you."

"Okay then, that is what we will do. I want to go by and see if I can get some tickets for 'Aunty Mame' if I can."

They went out for a nice lunch and Anne said "Rob, I have a favor to ask of you. Well, I guess it isn't exactly a favor, I just want to ask if it is okay to change the plan a bit."

"You name it, Mrs. Darcel, and I'll make it happen if I can."

"Well before I go any further with my question, would you mind to call me Anne? I think if we are going to be family, we need to be a little less formal, don't you?"

"That would be great, Anne. Now what can I do to make you happy?"

"Well you see, I met a very nice couple who live here in New York and a very nice single gentleman with whom I played bridge a lot. We found we had a lot in common and really enjoyed each other's company. They asked if I could go out with them tomorrow night and I would really like to do that. That would leave you and Renee free to have your first real date alone and I think that is the way it should be. I am mentioning this now so that you won't go ahead and buy a ticket for me. Is that okay with you"?

"It is more than okay, Anne. I think that is great that you made some friends. While we would be very happy to have you with us, I know that you will enjoy getting to see them all again. Now, we will leave you to your nap and to contact your friends and make whatever plans you want to for the time we are here.

Meanwhile, we will take off and do some sightseeing. Shall we meet in the hotel dining room at eight in the morning for breakfast?"

"Sounds good. You all have fun."

"We will, thanks. Let's wait here for the valet to bring the car around. I thought we would drive around and just see parts of the city later but there is one thing I would like to do yet today. Tiffany's is not very far away so I would like to go there first. There is a very important gift I need to buy for my most special girl in the world. Oh, here is the car right now."

They parked the car in a special parking lot for customers only and went in to the most fabulous jewelry store Renee had ever seen in her life. The most gorgeous china and crystal and diamonds were everywhere she looked in one form or another--bracelets, watches and rings. Then it dawned on her. Rob was getting ready to buy her a ring!

"Now, Sweets, I want you to look at the wedding sets and see if you find something you really like."

"Oh Rob, they are all so beautiful. I don't think I could ever choose one among so many."

"Well, let's do it like this. I will put five in front of you, and you put them in the order of preference. Then we will eliminate two. You can choose the best two out of three and then maybe you can make a final decision."

"Okay, that sounds like a good plan. But, Rob, I want to give you a ring also, so shouldn't you be looking at some too?"

"As a matter of fact, Renee, these sets come with wedding rings for both the bride and groom so we are picking them out together. That way, our rings will match."

"Oh, that is great."

After going through the selection process, they decided on a gorgeous platinum ring set with a beautiful solitaire surrounded by baguettes and smaller diamonds for the engagement ring and for both wedding rings a band with diamonds all across the top.

"Are you sure this is the one you want?"

"Yes. Are you also happy with it?"

"Very happy. As a matter of fact, I had been in here before because I had some time to kill waiting for you to arrive so I picked out those five sets as being the ones I liked best. And you won't believe this, but the one you picked is the one I had as first choice."

"He's right, Miss." said the clerk. "I was the one who showed them to him and he told me the one he liked best and you picked it too. Now shall I write this up for you?"

"Absolutely. Let's check the sizes for both of us and make sure they are right."

After the sizes were checked, the purchase made and the parcel was handed to Rob, he said, "Sweets, if it is all right with you, I want to give you this ring in a more appropriate setting, so you can't have it now."

"Oh, I agree completely. Can we go someplace quickly that is appropriate?" she said as she smiled and squeezed his arm.

Rob laughed and hugged her to him with the arm he had around her. "Of course we can, my darling. But it will have to be the hotel if it is very quick. Like my room. Okay? I don't really think your Mom will mind too much if we spend some time in my room alone. She knows I will take very good care of you. After all, I am going to have that job the rest of our lives and I can tell you right now, I can't wait to begin my new position."

"That sounds so wonderful to me. I want to take care of you too. At least I know how to cook and keep house as that is something my Mother insisted on Ria and I both learning to do. She said when she got married, she didn't know how to do anything and it was very hard on her and my Dad too."

"That is great. Did I tell you I like to cook too? I think we will have fun cooking together."

"Oh, that will be wonderful. Then we will find out what each other likes at the same time, or doesn't like" she said, smiling.

"Right. Oh, here is our car. Let me help you in."

They got in the car, drove to the hotel and turned the car over to the valet again. They got on the elevator and went to Rob's room. He said "now you sit in that chair right there." And he proceeded to kneel down in front of her and said "Sweets, I know you have already said you love me and have agreed on the phone to be my wife, but I want to see you when I propose and when you answer. I want to put the ring on your finger. Call me old fashioned, but that is the way I have always imagined I would do it."

As he knelt, he said to her, "Sweets, you have been in my life one way or the other for about three years and I can honestly say, I have never had a nicer, sweeter, friend and I could never find anyone I am more in love with than you. I think I may have been in love with you all the time too but I thought you were too young for me and I didn't allow myself to admit it. But at least we are past that and I am asking you now. I love you with all my heart, Renee Darcel., will you be my wife?"

"Oh yes, I will Rob and I will love you forever".

So Rob put the ring on her finger and they spent the next hour or two making up for lost time. Renee was getting so excited she was losing her breath and Rob was getting very aroused so he said, "it is time to cool it for now, Sweets. We will have plenty of time to do things right at the right time. Okay?"

"Yes, I am sure you're right. I know there are things we need to discuss so this is a good time to do it, don't you think?"

"An excellent time. Now let's just sit here with a pad and pencil, I happen to have handy, and write down things we need to do to get our wedding planned. I hope you won't feel too bad that Mom and I have talked about some things already, since we have so little time to plan and actually have it if we schedule it while your Mom is there."

"Oh, I don't mind at all. I know how much there is to do for even a small wedding since I've just finished helping Ria do hers."

"Okay then, we'll do a little sightseeing in New York and if you want to shop some, you can."

"Oh weren't we supposed to pick up the tickets at the Tickethon while we were out today?"

"You are right! I got so excited about the ring and wanting to put it on that I forgot that. I had also forgotten that you said you would like to do some shopping tomorrow, we will; But, for now, let's have a nice lunch and have a late dinner just before going to see the show. I am not usually so forgetful; I am just too excited to think straight. On second thought, I think I will just stop by the desk at the hotel and see if I can order the tickets and save us a trip."

"I am having trouble thinking straight too as I am so excited to be here with you".

'I know, Sweets, and isn't it wonderful?" as he squeezed her arm.

Could we possibly go up to our room and show Mama my ring? I just can't wait for her to see it."

"Of course, sweetheart. Why don't you go on up there and I will stop by the desk and see if I can order the tickets and then I will join you in a few minutes."

Renee went to their room and knocked but there was no answer. She used her card and opened the door. The light was on and there was a note on the desk from her mom, saying that Gordon and Meg Brown and Brandon Scott called and asked her to go to dinner with them. She said not to wait up that they might play some bridge.

Renee smiled to herself. "Hmm--I think there might be more to this friendship than any of us thought."

About that time, Rob knocked on the door and he agreed with Renee that something was going on with this Brandon fellow.

'Oh, he is a very nice man, Rob. The Browns are lovely people too. It seems they have been friends with Brandon and his wife for many years. They continue to see each other although not very often since he lost his wife three years ago. That is about the same time we lost my Dad so I guess that is something Mama and Brandon have in common."

"Well, I guess we can continue our planning session. Let's go back to my suite and we'll get room service for our dinner. How would you like that? Oh yes, I was able to order the tickets and they will deliver them to the hotel for us. That will be better than waiting in line to pick them up at the door."

"Oh yes, much better. I am not very hungry, Rob. Just order a salad for me, please."

When their food came and they ate, Rob got his pencil and pad out again and started their list. "Now some of the first things we have to do when we get to Dallas is to go get our blood tests, buy our marriage license, contact the Minister to get on his schedule, order our invitations and make an appointment with the Caterer and florist."

"Is the church building very large? Will it be difficult to decorate? The one at home was rather small and Ria and her new sister-in-law, along with a little help from me, did it all."

"Well, yes, it is quite large. There is an alternative, however.

Mom and Dad have offered their beautiful back yard garden to have our wedding if you would like to have it there. If you prefer to have it in church, we will do that.

In any case, we will definitely have a Minister to perform it. My sister, Eileen, had her wedding in the garden there at home.

She had an archway for the bride and groom to stand in front of and all decorated with flowers; it was really beautiful."

"It sounds lovely. It is very nice of your family to offer. I think I can already say I'd love a garden wedding. It sounds so glamorous."

"Only if you want to, Sweetheart. This is our wedding and I want you to be perfectly happy with it. Mom has phone numbers for florists and caterers and there's a stationery store that does wedding invitations close to my office. I know the man who owns it and he will give us a fair deal and a quick one which is what we need."

"So, if you want the garden wedding, the Caterer will furnish a large tent and everything including furniture, dishes, silver, food, wedding cake for a sit-down dinner to accommodate up to 100 guests. We will, of course, select the wedding cake and the food and tell them the color scheme we want. The Florist will coordinate the flowers you select for decoration for the archway which they will provide, if you want it, so that not only the wedding but also the reception will be there."

"That sounds like the way to go. I like it already."

"Well darling, it is getting late and you have had very little rest so I am going to walk you to your room, kiss you goodnight and let you get some sleep. I will drop by and pick you up around eight for breakfast instead of meeting you in the Dining Room. Okay?"

"Sounds fine to me. I am getting a bit sleepy as I hardly slept a wink last night just thinking about seeing you. I don't whether I can stand to wait until morning to see you again. I am so excited that I can't think straight. It is like I'm in a dream and if it is, I hope I never wake up."

"It's not a dream, Sweetheart, but it is going to be heaven being with you. Not to mention getting to claim you for mine alone and having you claim me for yours alone too." He then reached over and squeezed her tight against him and kissed her.

"I agree, Rob. I can hardly wait for that too and I am very anxious to meet your parents."

"They are very anxious too. You can't know how thrilled they are that I have finally fallen in love and am to be married soon. Now they are even talking about grandchildren not only to me but they've been talking like that to Eileen ever since she got married about two years ago," he continued, laughing. "Incidentally, how do you feel about children?"

"I adore them. I definitely want to have a family. How about you? Of course, we've never talked about that but we have talked about a lot of other things."

"Yes, we surely have, and I think it is a definite advantage being good friends first; however, we have so many more things to find out about each other and I am looking forward to knowing everything about you. I am so glad you feel the same way I do about a family, Sweets. I have always wanted a family when I get married.

We've had a happy family and I'd like to think I could make a happy home for children too. I would love it if we had at least one boy and one girl. Of course, I understand that you can't order by sex so you take what is sent to you. But that is okay. I can live with all girls or all boys too."

"Me too. We definitely agree on family." I want to know everything about you too. I want to make you happy."

'You are already making me happy and I feel very sure that we are going to be very happy together." he said with a big hug.

"Well here we are at your room. Goodnight, my love."

He held her tight and kissed her forehead then each cheek and then a long sweet kiss on her lips. Renee was thrilled to her toes.

"Goodnight, Rob darling. See you in the morning."

Next morning, Rob got up showered, shaved, and dressed and was all ready to go pick up the girls. He phoned first to see if they were ready and they said they would be in about five minutes. So he sauntered on down to their room after waiting about three minutes and knocked on the door.

Renee opened the door and she was dressed in an adorable white eyelet capri set with white sandals. Her long dark brown hair was pulled back in a pony tail and Rob's heart was in his throat just looking at how beautiful she was. She had such gorgeous blue-gray eyes and long black lashes and a rosebud mouth. "Hello my angel. My, don't you look pretty! Come here, I want to give you a good morning kiss." Which he did and received a very warm response. "Is your Mom about ready too?" "Yes, she's just finishing up in the bathroom."

When Anne came out, she looked very nice in a blue linen summer suit with matching shoes and purse. "You look lovely Anne. Did you have a nice evening with your friends?" "I certainly did. We had a delicious Italian dinner and then went over to the Brown's beautiful home and played bridge until very late. Renee was sound asleep when I came in. I love her beautiful ring. It is simply gorgeous."

"Well that is great. We made good use of the time and made some headway. We will be going to the show tonight. of course. We will leave for Dallas tomorrow afternoon. Our flight leaves about 2:20 so we should be at the airport no later than 1:30. I hope that is okay with you."

"That will be fine. I will be ready."

While they were eating breakfast, they started talking about what they should do first. Rob said he wanted to take them to the Empire State Building and to Rockefeller Center and to Central Park, at least. He also wanted to take them to a special Deli for lunch that was famous and at which he had eaten and liked it very much.

Anne looked up and said, "well I hope you won't be disappointed if I don't join you. Since I have plans for the evening with Brandon and the Browns, they have invited me to spend the day with them sightseeing, going to lunch, and whatever else we decide to do. I hope that is okay with you two. I know you have so much to say to each other and I am enjoying my new friends very much. Too, this is probably the last time I will see them."

"That would be just fine with me, Mama. I am glad you are having such a great time."

"I agree, Anne. You should take advantage of having a good time with people you enjoy. I will just bet that this isn't the last time you see them." Rob said, teasingly.

Anne smiled and said "Well let's put it this way. There are no future plans."

After breakfast, Anne went on back to the suite to await her friends and Rob and Renee went out and requested the car so they could get on with their sightseeing. They were able during the day to take in all three things Rob had mentioned and by the time they had finished, they were both exhausted.

They stopped by the Deli Rob had mentioned and Renee agreed it was great. Rob suggested that they rest for awhile so they went to the suite and sat down with a cool glass of iced tea they ordered sent up and just talked.

They had discussed their likes and dislikes in food, beverages, movies, TV shows, colors, music and sports and were surprised to find they had many things in common. Renee said she didn't like to watch sports on TV but that she didn't mind if Rob did. He said he definitely liked the Cowboys.

After that, Rob said he had a couple of serious things to talk to her about. Renee said to go ahead. "Well we got the important discussion about family out of the way or sort of, however, we didn't talk about family planning. I would like to suggest that we postpone having our family for at least a couple of years. That will allow time for my business to grow and for us to have selected and bought a home if that's what we decide to do. How do you feel about that?"

"I definitely agree, Rob. I think every couple should have some time alone, if possible, before having a family. I also realize that it doesn't always work out like that, but that is okay too, if it happens that way."

"I agree. I want to talk about finances too. Renee, I want to give you everything possible to make things convenient and happy for you. My business is going very well and I have an ample income to accomplish that, I think. First of all, lets's agree to decide together about making all major purchases, like furniture and our home or cars. That does not mean you have to ask permission to spend money on things you need or want. We will have a checking account for you to use for the household and any spending money you need. We will also have a savings account which we will add to each month, hopefully, to save for buying our home. We will also set aside some for entertainment. Does that sound like a good arrangement to you?"

"Yes, I do agree on that. But, Rob, I don't mind getting a job too so that I can help you save for our home. Of course, I haven't ever had but one job and that has been in the café where

I met you. I can do other things like typing and filing which I took in high school. Unfortunately, I haven't had any training or experience in a business office, which I know pays more and is what I would really like to do. I was told once by a gentleman who used to come into the café that I would make a good receptionist as I was friendly and could talk easily to people. Do you think I might get a job like that?"

I think you can do anything you really want to do, sweetheart. But, I would like to tell you first of all that it won't be necessary financially for you to work. I want you to do what you want to do, so I will not object if that will make you happy. However, I have a suggestion for you to think about. We'll discuss it fully when the time comes, but how would you like to go to college or enroll in some kind of formal training? There are many options and I am prepared to make this possible for you if you want to do it. I can remember in our talks, you have expressed your wish to go to college. If you still have that desire, let's do something about it."

'Oh, Rob, I never dreamed I'd ever have a chance to do anything but be a Waitress. I" have always thought I would love to be an Executive Secretary. I've also thought it would be fun being a Court Reporter."

"Well, we will look into it after we get back from our honeymoon and are moved and settled into our apartment. That will be awhile as we will have furniture and household items to select and purchase. Unless, of course, we decide on a furnished apartment first which would allow us to take our time on our furniture selections." We will also need to buy a car for you so that you can get around to do things you want and need to do."

"Oh, Rob, I hate to tell you this but I have never learned to drive. We had only the one car and Mama had to use it for work so I never learned. Ria finally got one when she started to work."

"Well, we can take care of that. I can teach you to drive. And we will get you a car."

"Oh that would be great."

"Another thing, Renee, that I haven't told you until now, I have been looking at apartments for the past few weeks and have found one that I think will be convenient for us not far from downtown Dallas and my office. It is close to shopping for most anything we would need as there is a large mall about two miles away. I have a hold on it, subject to your approval. If you don't really like it, we will find something else. I want to stress to you that I want you to be honest about your feelings so that I can learn to sense them. I don't want you to be shy about suggesting things or disagreeing with me if you feel strongly about something. I want to feel free to do the same. Okay"

"Okay, I promise. I am not really very hard to please, Rob. I have had very few important decisions to make so I will just have to learn to do it as I go along."

"Well, I want you to make your first one when we get to Dallas. I'd like to leave the decision on what flowers we have for our wedding up to you. Mom and your mom will go with you to help, but I will not need to help with that. I need to go to my office half days for the next week. I will go in the mornings so that we have the afternoons to go together to do the things we need to do. Will you do that?"

"Oh yes, I am sure that I can, especially if our moms are with me. I think it will be fun to help plan the decorations for the garden, the tables and the house. I am so excited I can hardly wait to get there and get things going."

"Me too, honey. Let's just try to enjoy tonight. I know we are a little bushed from today's activities, but I think you will really like the show. Incidentally, we should both get our showers and get dressed so we can get on out to dinner and be on time for it. I'll walk you to your room now so you can get started."

Anne was having such a good time with her new friends that the day had gone by rapidly. They had gone sightseeing, out to lunch and then back to the Browns for a little rest and relaxation.

I do wish you didn't have to leave tomorrow," said Meg to Anne as they were fixing a tray of snacks and cold drinks in the kitchen. I don't know if you've noticed, but Brandon wishes you weren't leaving also."

"Well, I can't tell you how much I have enjoyed being with all of you. The time has passed so quickly, and yet, I feel I have known you for a long time." Brandon is very charming and I, too, wish I had a bit more time."

"That's the way we feel too. Since you said you are flying home, why don't you come just a few days early and stop off here and stay the time with us? We'll get Brandon to come back too. And from the way things look between you two, I don't think it will take any coaxing from us" she said, with a grin.

"I would like to do that, but I will just have to see what I can do about it. I do want us to stay in touch for I feel I have made some fine new friends. As far as Brandon is concerned, he is such a great person to be around. He is very sincere and down-to-earth and so well spoken. I love to hear his voice and yes, I like him very much. I can't believe I have known him for only a week. We don't ever run out of something to say to each other."

"Well, believe me, you are the first person that Brandon has ever given the time of day to, since his wife's death. Of course, a lot of his friends are always trying to arrange a date for him with someone, but he just hasn't been interested. He told Gordon that you are the first person that he's met that he has been really interested in getting to know. He also told him he was planning on a trip to Europe, probably this fall, and that he intends to see you."

"He did mention that he would do that. I will look forward to seeing him again. Why don't you and Gordon plan to come too?"

"Hmm--sounds tempting. We'll have to see about that."

"Do you ever think about getting married again, Anne?"

"Well. I can't say it hasn't crossed my mind. Although, I haven't had anyone in mind. I'll admit it has been somewhat lonely, at times. Of course, I have had the girls with me and we have always done a lot of things together. But that is going to change with both girls getting married within a month of each other and leaving home. It will be especially hard with Renee so far away. I will see Ria often as she will be living in the same town. But even that will be different than having her live at home."

"I understand that very well. Both our son and daughter are married and live in different states. It is really hard on us since we now have a grandson from one and a granddaughter from the other. But we manage to see them all occasionally, especially since Gordon has retired."

"That does make it easier. Of course, I still work full time and feel fortunate to have a good job, not only for my income, but I enjoy my friends there and my work too."

"Well, I guess the guys are wanting their drinks and snacks, so we'd better get back in there. Here we come, bearing food and drinks. Speaking of food, where are you gentlemen taking us for dinner tonight?"

"We were just discussing that. What do you think about a real American dinner? Prime Rib with Baked Potato and all the trimmings?" How about you Anne?"

"It sounds wonderful to me. I seem to like all of your food over here, so far. I will have to go on a diet when I get home for sure," she said, laughingly.

"You will hardly need to do that, Anne," said Brandon. "I think you will like this place, however. We've been there. It is a Supper Club and they have a great live band and show. There is also dancing for those who want to do so."

'Sounds great to me" Anne said, as she smiled at Brandon.

"I'm all for it too, dittoed Meg. We should be through with dinner and the show about 10 o'clock. How about if we come back here for dessert? I just made a strawberry cheesecake and we'll have coffee and visit a little more before the evening ends."

"Sounds great to me, hon. How about you, Brandon and you, Anne?"

"Okay with me" chimed in Brandon, followed by the same from Anne.

Rob stopped by and knocked on Renee's door. When she came to the door, he just gasped at her. "You look absolutely fabulous, Sweets. I love the way you have put your hair up. That outfit makes you look like you came right out of Vogue."

"Thank you, kind sir. You don't look so bad yourself."

Rob smiled and said "and thank you, my darling girl. Shall we let the mutual admiration society leave for dinner and a night out?"

The dinner and the stage play were both very special. The food and service were impeccable and Renee just knew she would never forget the stage play. She told Rob she would dream of seeing that play over and over again. The costumes were simply beautiful and it was such a treat to see live actors. It was late when they got home and they were both exhausted from such a full day.

"We'd better say goodnight, as we have another full day tomorrow, traveling to the great state of Texas," Rob said as he took Renee in his arms and kissed her soundly in front of her hotel room. She was practically asleep as she was so tired so they said good night and he opened the door for her and left for his room.

The Browns, Brandon and Anne got back to the Brown's home around 10:30. Meg made coffee and they all sat at the kitchen table and had some with dessert. They all agreed what a great time they had together on the cruise and since they'd been in New York. They all agreed, too, that they would keep in touch and try to see each other again.

Anne and Brandon said goodnight and left for Anne's hotel. As they approached her suite, Brandon said "Anne, I can't possibly tell you what the last few days have meant to me. I feel as if I have known you for a long time, and yet, I keep wanting to know you even better. Will you write to me? I would really like that so we can keep in touch. I will see you again, if you want me to. Count on that."

"I feel the same way, Brandon. You are so easy to talk with and have such interesting things to tell. I would like to get to know you better too and yes, I will correspond with you. I will be looking forward to your coming to France on your trip abroad this Fall. Well, here we are at the hotel. Just let me out. Since you have to park, I will just go on up."

"I don't mind at all, but I know you are tired. May I give you a kiss goodnight and goodbye?

"Yes, you may." She leaned over and he put his arms around her and gave her a very sweet, romantic kiss. It was very obvious that something great was happening between them with that kiss and Brandon said, "do you think we could meet for breakfast tomorrow? I just can't let you go with one kiss."

"Yes, let's do. Why don't you come over around eight o'clock. We'll have breakfast with the kids as I want you to meet Rob. Then you and I will spend an hour or so together before we leave for the airport. Would that be okay?"

"Great. Goodnight, my dear."

"Goodnight, Brandon. Thanks for a lovely day and evening."

"It was my pleasure. See you tomorrow."

When Anne got in, she peeked into Renee's bedroom and found that she was fast asleep. She got undressed and cleaned her face and brushed her teeth and settled into bed, but for some reason, she just wasn't sleepy. She didn't want to watch TV or read.

What she did do, however, was think of Brandon. The kiss was very sweet and gave her very unsettled feelings in her stomach and, well, all over, as a matter of fact.

After all, it had been three years since she had experienced a romantic kiss, because she had not been interested in even going out on a date since her husband, Bill, had been killed. They had been very much in love and she had doubted if she could ever have feelings for another man. Since she had met Brandon, she wasn't so sure. She tossed and turned and thought some more and finally about 2:30 AM, she went to sleep.

The next thing she knew Renee was calling her to get up and get dressed to go to breakfast. Rob came by and got them and when they got to the Dining Room, there was Brandon waiting for them. Anne couldn't help noticing what a fine looking gentleman he was. Rob gave her a kiss on the cheek and she introduced Brandon.

They had a nice leisurely breakfast and then started talking about the Newspaper Business and the Accounting Business. Brandon said his son, John, was doing a great job carrying on the business since he retired and that he had been spending a lot of time traveling since then.

Rob and Renee got up to leave as they wanted to get their things packed for their trip to Dallas that afternoon. They shook hands with Brandon and Anne said she would be on up in a few minutes.

After they left, Brandon reached over and kissed her goodbye and gave her a telephone number to call him to let him know when she arrived in Dallas. He said when she has a phone number to give him, he will do the calling. They reluctantly said goodbye and she went on upstairs to do her packing.

After they checked in at the airport, Rob said, "Brandon seems to be a very nice guy. He is an interesting man too. I think I would like him if I get to know him better."

"I think you would, Rob. He is a very nice man. We have had a very good time together these past few days."

"Maybe he can come down for our wedding. Isn't he only in Joplin, Missouri? That's not too far at all."

'Well, I don't know what his plans are, but we can certainly ask him if you both want him to. It would be nice to see him again before I go home to France."

"Oh Mama. I think that would be great. I really like him and especially if being with him makes you happy."

"Well, let's not read something into it prematurely. I enjoy his company and I know he does mine and that is all there is to it."

"If you say so" said Rob with a wink and a smile.

The trip to Dallas was long and by the time they got there, it was late and they were very tired. When they were down in the baggage room, Rob made a call and got a limo to pick them up out front. A sky cap took their luggage and put it in the car. When they got to Rob's parents' home, Renee gasped at what a large and beautiful place it was. It had such a long driveway, she thought they would never see the house.

His parents were waiting to greet them. They both shook hands with Anne and warmly welcomed her. Rob kissed his mother and gave his Dad a pat on the shoulder and said, "Mom and Dad, may I present the sweetest girl in the world, my future bride and your newest daughter-to-be?"

And then his mother said to Renee, "welcome, my dear, to our home and to our family" and gave her a warm hug. Jim Farnsworth, likewise, gave her a hug and said, "Rob said you were beautiful and you certainly are, my dear. We are so glad to have you here and in our family. I also see where you get your good looks. Welcome, Mrs. Darcel."

"Thank you. It is very nice of you to have us in your home."

At that, Janet turned to Anne and said "it is our pleasure. We know how tired you must be so come with me and I will show you to your rooms. All of you just sleep as late as you wish in the morning. We will have plenty of time to get acquainted tomorrow."

"Sounds good, Mom. I'm beat and I am sure both Anne and Renee are too. Why don't you just let me show them to their rooms as I will need to take their luggage up, anyway. By the way, I am staying over tonight also."

"That's fine dear, your room is always ready. You know that."

"I'll give you a hand son, said his Dad." "Okay, Dad. Thanks. Good night Mom."

"Good night to you all."

"Good night to you too" Renee and Anne said in unison.

Rob gave Renee a kiss goodnight when he showed her to her room and put her luggage down. "See you in the morning, Sweets."

"Goodnight, Rob. Sleep well."

"You too, my darling".

Jim Farnsworth put Anne's luggage in her room and she thanked him and they said good night. Anne went to sleep as soon as her head touched the pillow.

After a good night's sleep and a refreshing shower, Anne, Renee, and Rob got dressed and went down to breakfast. Jim and Janet were sitting there with newspapers and coffee. They greeted each other warmly and Jim said, "How about some coffee now and in a few minutes a real Texas breakfast?"

"Sounds wonderful to me" Anne said as she helped herself to coffee and sat down beside Janet.

"Me too", chimed Renee.

Rob poured coffee for him and Renee and then he said, "Eat a good breakfast, Sweets, for you and I have a lot of things to do today."

"I know, and I can't wait to get started." and she smiled her warmest smile for him.

"What all are you two up to today?" asked Janet.

"Well we have tried to prioritize our list so that we get as much done as possible today. We are going to go get blood tests and our license first. Then, we are to see the Minister at 1:00 o'clock today. If we can get a firm date on his schedule, then we will go directly to the stationers' and order our invitations."

"And, oh yes, Mom, I guess we forgot to discuss this since Renee and Anne have been here, but Renee said she would love to have a garden wedding. So, if you haven't changed your mind, we would like to have it here. Also, you and Anne are elected to help Renee make all decisions concerning flowers and decorations. Is that okay with you ladies?"

"Absolutely all right; I have already thought a little bit about it, just in case you decided to have it here. I think this is just wonderful. Eileen's wedding was so pretty and went off so well there. Don't you think so, Jim?"

"Yes, it was lovely, dear and I am pleased Rob and Renee want to have theirs here too. It makes it so nice to be able to have the wedding and reception in the same place."

"How about you, Anne, since you have seen the garden outside?"

"Yes, I took a look outside when I first got up. It is lovely and I think it will be beautiful. I am excited about helping to decorate."

Maude, who had been their cook for many years, had the sideboard loaded with fresh fruit, sweet rolls, muffins, butter and assorted jam. The electric hot plate had sausages, bacon, and ham, hash brown potatoes and scrambled eggs. More hot fragrant coffee and chilled fresh orange juice was also available.

They all sat down to this hearty breakfast and began to get acquainted. One of the first things they did was to establish the rule of first names. They were to use the names, Anne, Janet, and Jim. Janet told Renee she could call them Mom and Dad if she liked. Since she used Mama for her own mother, she said she would like that and her Mom also thought it was nice. They had a great time establishing family names and relationships and were told they would meet Eileen and her husband, Keith, soon. They were also introduced to their friend and long-time cook, Maude Baldwin.

After everyone had finished eating and the ladies were clearing the table away, Rob looked over at Renee and said, "Are you up for a whirlwind today, Sweets?"

"I'm up for whatever you want to do. Did you say we were going to go to your office, too?"

"Yes, I should see about any important messages I might need to check on and too, I would really like to show off my bride-to-be to my staff."

Oh Rob, I had better wear something different in that case, shouldn't I?"

"Of course not, you look adorable in that shorts outfit with your sandals. That's what people wear in Texas in summer time. Believe me, you look just perfect."

With the clearing over, Anne and Janet went out to the patio overlooking the garden and discussed some ideas they would present to Renee about the flowers and decorations. Jim had a golf game, so he left.

Rob and Renee went to the clinic lab to get their blood tests. That finished, they went to the county court house and got their marriage license. They were told that, since Renee had a visitor's visa, everything was in order from that standpoint, for them to go ahead and get married. She would need to apply for a green card if she were to plan to work or establish citizenship later.

They stopped by Rob's office which, to Renee, was very impressive. She was introduced to his two male accountants and one female accountant in addition to his administrative assistant, Katie, an attractive older lady. They were all very pleasant to her and asked her to call them by their first names, George, Mike, and Karen. Rob checked with Katie to see if there was anything he needed to do before leaving. He made one quick telephone call and gave some instructions to Katie and they were off again.

By this time, it was well after noon and time to go to see Craig Thornton, the Minister. Craig had been a high school friend of Rob's sister, who was about three years older than Rob. Their families were friends so they went over to their home instead of the Church. Lynn Thornton, Craig's wife, answered the door and Rob kissed her on the cheek and introduced Renee. Lynn was a very neat and pleasant lady and welcomed Renee to Texas and especially to Dallas.

Craig came in, with his pipe in his teeth, unlit as usual. And smiling, came over to Renee and took her hand and patted it with the other and said how glad he was that Rob had finally decided to join the group and get married. He said "we are so glad to meet you and I know that you can't help but be happy with a family like the Farnsworths." He gave Rob a playful shove and Renee immediately felt at ease with them.

They talked about a date and it was decided that they would have the wedding on June 24 in the Farnsworth garden. They said their goodbyes and when they were back in the car, Rob leaned over and gave Renee a long, sweet kiss and then said:

"I have an idea let's get some takeout lunch and go to my apartment to eat it. I want you to see where I currently live. Then after we've eaten, we will go to the stationers and see how soon we can get our invitations."

"Oh that sounds great, Rob. I am getting butterflies with all the things we are doing to get our life together started. I would love to see where you live. Is it large enough for us to just live there?"

"It is normal, I'm told, to get nervous about getting married. I guess it hasn't hit me yet, because I am just anxious. To answer your question about the apartment, yes, it is large enough. However, it is a furnished apartment and I thought you would probably want our own things."

"We will talk about it after you see it. I have this other place on hold until we go see it tomorrow and you should see them both before you decide which one you'd prefer."

"Okay, sounds good. What shall we get? How about Chinese?"

"Good choice. As a matter of fact, there's one not too far from my apartment."

They picked up the food and went to the apartment to eat. It was a very nice apartment building with an elevator and Rob's apartment had two bedrooms, two baths with a small kitchen, a nice-sized dinette and an adequate living room. The furniture was all modern and very pleasant.

As they ate their food, Renee told him she liked his apartment and that she wouldn't mind if they lived here. Rob asked her to wait until she saw the other one before she decided which place she wanted to live.

They spent a little time holding each other close and kissing until Rob suddenly said, "well we'd better leave and go see about the invitations."

After about an hour of looking at the various prints, fonts, and colors available, they decided on the one they both liked and John Stewart, the owner, promised to get them done in three days.

"That is just great, John. I can't tell you how much I appreciate your getting them done on such short notice."

"It is my pleasure, Rob. I am so glad to meet you, Renee, and I wish both of you every happiness."

"You too, John and my thanks to you also. Of course, I can't wait to see them."

"Okay Rob, everything is signed and we'll soon be ready to start printing."

"Please call when they are ready as I would like to pick them up."

"Sure thing, Rob. I'll get them out for you in a hurry."

When they got in the car, Rob said, "let's go look at the apartment."

"Oh yes, let's do."

The apartment complex had four apartments in each building, brick on the outside and very impressive. They got inside, with the help of the neighbor who had the key and was showing the apartment. Renee gasped with delight at how beautifully decorated it was.

The living room was spacious, featuring a white brick fireplace. The rugs in the house were a beautiful royal blue. It had beautiful drapes in blue and gold satin and there were perky little yellow curtains in the all-electric kitchen with a large pantry and island in the middle. The island had four stools upholstered in black leather. All the fixtures were black and the kitchen cabinets in white. The floor tile was black and white and the counter tops all black Corian.

There were two master suites. The main master bedroom had a Jacuzzi tub and both bedrooms had walk-in closets. The dining room had an elegant crystal chandelier. There were lacy white Priscilla curtains in the dining room and shades of blue drapes with white panels in both bedrooms. It was a sight to behold and Renee loved it at once.

"Well Sweets, what do you think? Do you like it?"

"Oh Rob, I just love it, but can we really afford it?"

"Yes, we can, although it will take us some time to select and buy our furniture. What kind do you like?"

"I really like French Provincial, of course. But do you like it? Be honest, like you tell me to be, Rob. I can be happy with anything as long as I am with you."

"Oh Renee, you are so funny but I love you for it. I honestly do like French Provincial, but, I also like Early American very much. We don't have to decide that right now, but I think either would look nice in this apartment.

"I have never seen Early American, but I would like to when we go shopping for furniture."

"Incidentally, they are building some great looking condos over near Irving, which makes this one look mediocre. They won't be ready for about six months, but they have a lot of amenities available to us that this one does not.

For instance, they have an indoor swimming pool so you can swim year round. They have an exercise room, a reading room and a game room. It is also on a golf course. They are also not very far from a great shopping mall which is being built at the same time. I would like to show you those if we can manage the time. There are a couple of problems, however."

"What's that?"

"Well, if we should take a lease on this one, we wouldn't be able to get out of it in time to get into the condos, as this one requires a two-year lease. The location of this one is very popular because it is in Dallas and not terribly far from the airport or downtown. I only have a hold on this one until next week, as they have a long waiting list of people wanting to move here. So we do have to make a decision."

"You sound like you would really like to go with the condos. Are they a lot more expensive than these?"

"They are more expensive, but considering all of the extra things they have to offer, they are worth it, I think. I have to admit that if they were available right now, I would choose them over these in a minute."

"Oh, I wish they were, because I want you to be happy with what we get. I know, why couldn't we just live in your apartment until the condos are ready? I think it is very nice and we wouldn't have to shop for furniture until later when we have plenty of time."

"Sweets, that is a great idea, if you are sure you want to do that. You are right. It would give us plenty of time to select our furniture and have them hold it until we are ready to move in. I know who to call about the condos so I will set up an appointment tomorrow afternoon so we can see them. Once they have assured us on paper that we will have a lease on the one we choose, we'll release the hold on this one."

"But what about the lease on the one where you live?"

"That is no problem. I have leased this one for two years and my lease was due to be renewed this month. I told the landlord I was getting married and wanted to let you select where we lived. I asked him if it was possible to lease by the month until we decide. He told me I could so that is what we will do.

Now, before we leave on our honeymoon, we will move all your things into my apartment, so that we will be all set when we return."

"That sounds wonderful to me. Of course, I only have three bags and a makeup case and hanging bag."

You will have a lot more by the time you have your wedding shower which one of Eileen's friends is giving for you."

"Oh, that's right and that is something else I have to do is to go with your Mom and Mama to establish our register. That is something new to me. I don't think we do that in France. It is really a very nice thing to do, though."

"Let's go home now and get that phone number so I can set up an appointment. Incidentally, honey, I have to go to the office in the morning. I will be home for lunch and then you and I will go do whatever we need to do. Our number one priority now is getting the Condo locked in, if it is what you want."

"That will be fine. Our Moms and I have an appointment with the florist."

"I remember that. You and I should make an appointment with the Caterer if possible after we get through seeing the apartment. I think we can do both."

They arrived at Rob's apartment and as they got out, Rob replied, "We probably can. If we can go to the Condos right after lunch, we would have the rest of the afternoon to do that."

He walked over to his desk and opened the front drawer and pulled out a business card. He punched in the number and in a few minutes, had set up an appointment for 1:30 the next day. Then he called another number and set up an appointment for 3;30 P.M. with the Caterer.

"That is just great. We can have the appointment. Renee, there is something else we need to think about. I'd like to have some nice music for our wedding and reception."

"Oh, I would too, Rob. Do you know anyone who could provide it? Ria happened to know a combo group who did hers."

"Well, as a matter of fact, my Dad has a bunch of friends who love to get together to play and they just look for opportunities to perform. If we invite them to the wedding, I am sure they will do it. We used them at Eileen's wedding and they were great. There's a cello, a violin, a flute, a sax, a bass fiddle, and drums, so they have a pretty good little orchestra."

"Sounds good. Can we get your Dad to handle that? I don't want him to feel left out of things."

"Great idea, Hon. Now you get together a list of the music you like and they will add in their own selections from classical to jazz."

"Well, I already know several I would choose. Mine would be the traditional wedding songs like 'Because' 'I Love you Truly' and 'Through the years'. Then I would like 'Clair de Lune', 'Oh Promise Me,' 'Long Ago and Far away' and 'Stranger on the Shore' as instrumentals."

"Sounds like we are ready to go on that score. They all sound good. We'll talk to Dad tonight and have him set it up."

"Before we leave, I need to call Lois McCall, who cleans for me. I told her she could clean for me while we are gone but now, I want her to empty a closet completely and a chest of drawers so that you have space to put your stuff before we leave."

Rob called Lois Mccall and she was very glad to change the schedule for cleaning. When he told her they would be living there for awhile, she asked if she might continue to work for him. He told her that hadn't been discussed but that he would get back with her on it.

"Rob, you mentioned that we would have a hotel after a few days here. I don't want your folks to feel an imposition, so could we set a time for that soon? I think, perhaps, it would make Mama feel better about it. Everyone has been wonderful to us, so don't think they haven't gone out of their way to make us welcome."

"I understand perfectly, Sweets. You need some time alone and Mom can pick the two of you up when you have appointments to keep or even if you need or just want to do something, we can make some transportation available. I want to see you everyday, however." "And I, you. In fact, I want to be with you every minute that you are not at the office if I can."

"Actually, I had planned to ask you about the hotel since I had previously mentioned it to you. It isn't necessary as I am sure you know, but I wanted to offer it if you did. I will call now and get it set up for this weekend. How would that be?"

"That will be great. That way, Mama can get used to the routine and can stay there until she leaves for home. She indicated she would plan to leave the next day after our wedding as she wants to spend a couple of days in New York before leaving for France. Oh, I forgot to tell you, Brandon Scott called her and said he would love to come to the wedding. He asked if we would make a hotel reservation for him where we would be staying. That is partly why I brought up the hotel subject."

"That is okay, honey. I will talk to her and confirm when she wants to leave for New York and when from there too so I can order her tickets."

"So, it looks like Mama and Brandon will be going to New York together."

"Sure does. How about that?"

When they arrived home, it was practically time for dinner, so they washed up and joined the family for a great Italian meal--Lasagne, Italian green beans, a huge tossed salad and toasted garlic bread. While they were eating, Rob said, "Dad, Renee and I would like to ask you to do something about the wedding."

"As long as you don't ask me to postpone it" he said, smiling and winking at Renee.

"Oh no, nothing like that. We want you to ask Bill and the other guys who play together to play at the wedding and reception. Tell them they can have all the food and drinks they want if they will play. Renee is working on a list of songs to give them."

"I feel that will be no problem at all. I think we would have to ask them to the wedding anyway, as they are all such old friends so they might as well work for it. They are always looking for places to perform and they thoroughly enjoyed getting to play for Eileen. I will be glad to take care of that for you."

"Thanks very much, Dad. I will get the list to you tomorrow. Did you notice I tried out my new name for you?"

"I surely did my dear, and I am very pleased. Anything I can do for you, you just ask." and he smiled broadly.

"Mom, I have something to ask you too. Do you think that Eileen would be my Matron of Honor? I am sure she has an appropriate dress for that sort of thing, already."

"I believe she would, Renee. Why don't you call and ask her yourself? Incidentally, I liked you trying out my name too" she said, with a twinkle in her eyes. "Her number is in the personal directory over there. Go ahead and call her now if you wish. Then you can mark that off your list too."

"Okay, I believe I will." She dialed the phone and then asked Eileen about being Matron of Honor. Eileen acted very pleased and asked what color dress she would like her to have. She asked if she, by any chance had a pastel blue or green dress.

Eileen told her she had a very pretty green one that was made a lot like the wedding dress so they decided on that. She would only need to shorten it to waltz length, however, and she said it was no problem.

"Well, that is one more thing we have settled. I want my Mother to give me away."

"I think that is wonderful, Renee, and as it should be."

The next morning, Rob said goodbye to everyone at the breakfast table and went to his office. Anne, Janet and Renee got ready and went to the florist. They selected the flowers for Renee's bouquet which would be baby pink roses, baby breath, green lacy fern and a white orchid in the center.

They selected baby roses and green fern for Eileen's bouquet. They would have green carnations for the men's boutonnieres. All types of colorful flowers were to be twined around the archway where they were to stand during the ceremony and small vases of flowers to be placed at each table in the large tent which the Caterer would supply.

"While we are at it, let's go to Neiman-Marcus and shop around for things to put on your gift register; then we will go to Macy's to do the same. There are a couple of kitchen stores where you will want to register at also. This helps your guests a lot in selecting gifts for you."

"I know it does. I had thought Rob should help me do that."

Rob, should and will, I am sure, help on it; however, knowing Rob, I am certain he will want you to make the final decisions on this type of thing. Like most all men, he really doesn't like to shop for things like that. I selected all of the stuff he has in his apartment," Janet said, laughing.

"Once you select it, they will give you a list and you can take it to show him what you decided and if he wants something different, you can discuss it. It takes quite a bit of time to do, and I am sure he will appreciate your doing this."

"I am sure you are probably right, based on some of our discussions. I haven't made many important decisions in my life, except one, and I am just going to have to learn."

"Renee, I agree with Janet. These are things that you will be the primary user of, so you should go ahead and pick things out you want to use." remarked her mother.

"Okay, let's do it. I want to be back home for lunch as Rob will be there to pick me up. We are going to go look at the new condos they are building near Irving."

"Oh, I hear those are going to be just lovely, dear. Do you know when they will be ready for occupancy?"

"Not for sure. That is one of the things we want to find out. The other thing we want to do is to see if it is where we want to live. We have another apartment that we've looked at which is available now and it is gorgeous. However, I already know that Rob would prefer the condo if it was available now, as he said so. We plan to make a decision today."

Anne had been silent up to this point. She now asked Janet, "how far are these condos they're talking about? Will it be convenient to Rob's office?"

"It is really between here and Irving and not too far, although it is very convenient to Rob's office, he says. I haven't actually seen them, myself, but I have a good idea where they are located."

They went to Neiman's and selected two possible patterns of silver, china, and crystal, all subject to Rob's final approval. They went to a kitchen store where Renee selected her cookware, everyday dishes, everyday stainless steel flatware, casserole dishes, pie and cake pans, cookie sheets, cooling racks and rolling pin.

Lastly, they went to a linen store and picked out towels, wash cloths, dish cloths, hot pads, sheets, pillow cases, place mats and bathroom accessories.

"We had better get on home now. Rob will be there about 12:30 and Maude will have lunch all ready for us."

Rob was extremely pleased that they had made the selections for household goods. He confessed that he didn't really like shopping for things like that. He didn't mind going with Renee to look at the things she wanted help with, however.

"As soon as we have lunch, if you are not too tired, we will go look at the Condos and get our decision made on where to live. Then, we will go and I will look at what you have selected and we'll make a final selection for the Register."

"It would be very helpful if you would have the Register ready from which people can chose their gifts. Eileen will make sure of the date and place and let you know. She would plan to pick us up and take us there."

"Oh, what a nice thing to do," said Anne.

"I agree, Mama. Of course, they are really doing it because they know the Farnsworths, because they don't even know me."

"But you are to be one of the Farnsworths too, my dear, and this is one of the traditional things to do for an engaged couple about to get married. It will also give all the girls a chance to get to know you and for you to know them. It will be a lot of fun, too" said Janet.

There will be games and prizes and delicious refreshments."

"Yum, I think I will go too," Rob said.

"Me too, said Jim, who had been quietly observing all the goings-on.

"Oh, no you won't--no men allowed," Janet said with a smile.

The condos were very spacious and they looked at plans for landscaping and were very impressed. The condos were to be fully decorated, together with the landscaping, the pool and all other amenities completed in four months, which would be in October The Golf Course was already there and in operation. They required a two-year lease and if decided on before decorating started, the lessee could select colors, flooring, carpeting, tile, woodwork, bathroom fixtures, appliances, cabinetry and window coverings.

"They are just beautiful, Rob. I really like them a lot."

"Shall we take the plunge and sign a lease? We will take home all of the literature and decide on colors and materials for decorating. I am told that will be the last thing they do, so we will have plenty of time."

"I think that would be wonderful. I know we will do just fine in your apartment until then. Oh, I am so excited. I know I will like living here."

"I think we will like it too, Sweets. I am glad we can pick out everything like we want it to look. It will be nice to be able to coordinate our furniture selections too."

"Yes, it will. I hadn't really thought of that. Of course, I have never had anything to do with decorating a house or an apartment."

"We will be able to ask for help in any problems if we need it."

Rob signed the lease. The Salesman handed them the complete portfolio containing all colors and materials available for selection, thanked them and said goodbye.

"Now what we have to do is to go by and release the apartment we had on hold and then go to my landlord and tell him you will be moving in and that we want at least a four-month lease. That way, we will be sure we have a place to stay until our condo is ready.

This took about another two hours and Renee was exhausted.

"Could we possibly stop someplace and rest awhile before going anyplace else? I feel like I have been on a treadmill."

You poor darling. I will bet you do, and we certainly can stop awhile. Let's get a soda and just relax a bit. You have really accomplished a lot today in making the decisions on flowers and decorations. They sound lovely and I also appreciate you asking Eileen to be in the wedding. We have always been close and I hope the two of you will be. I am really glad you took time to pick out the Register Lists, also."

"I hope you will like my choices. I just have to insist on your helping me make the final decision on the china, crystal and silver so I have narrowed in down to two patterns of each you so it shouldn't be too difficult."

"I am sure I will like whatever you like. I promise to help you on those since you were so nice to excuse me from picking out all the other stuff."

"Thanks, that will be great. How did work go today? I'm sorry, I have been too pre-occupied to even ask you."

"As a matter of fact, it went extremely well. We landed a large account that we've been working on for the last two months. We signed a contract this morning."

"I would normally take the new client to lunch, but I told them I already had an important engagement, so I asked George, Mike, and Karen to do it. They seemed pleased that I asked them. They also teased me and told me they knew who I had an important engagement with" he said, laughing.

"That's great. I'll bet you are a very nice boss."

"I do try to be fair and honest. That is the way I was taught to be."

"That is pretty obvious, seeing how nice your parents are. I just love them both."

"And they just love you too, my pretty girl. We are going to be so happy. Why am I saying 'going to be?' I am so happy now I can hardly see straight. I just kept looking at my watch while waiting for you to disembark and thinking how long it had been before since I saw your sweet face again."

"I was watching the time too. I have to pinch myself every now and then to believe all of the happiness that is being given to me. I hope I deserve it for I do love you so."

"You deserve to have everything that will make you happy and I intend to do everything in my power to see that you are for you know how much I love you too."

"I know you will Rob. I feel the same way about you."

"Well, do you think you are rested enough to go see the Caterer now?"

"Yes, I am fine now. I just needed a little breather, I believe you call it."

They went to see the Caterer, decided on the large tent, complete with ten tables to seat eight at each one, a large table for the wedding cake, and a punch bowl. They picked a three-tiered white cake with lemon filling decorated in pink roses and pale green leaves.

They chose shrimp cocktail, roasted prime rib of beef, twice-baked potatoes, asparagus with hollandaise sauce and Caesar salad for the sit-down dinner menu.

The Caterer was also to furnish the Archway to be decorated by the Florist. They, of course, would supply all silver, china, crystal, glassware, and table linens, as well.

"I don't think we forgot anything, do you?" "No. I can't possibly think of anything else."

"Well, let's go home now and rest up before dinner. Your Mom indicated to me that she would like to go to the hotel tomorrow so I need to make a call for that. Is that okay with you? You know you don't either one have to move at all as far as my folks are concerned. I understand your Mom's need for some privacy, however."

"She just wants to make sure your Mother doesn't feel she has to include us in everything she does. If she wants us to do something, all she has to do is to call. She does understand that, I hope."

"Yes, I am sure she does."

"Another thing I have to do is to make reservations for the Rehearsal Dinner. I have found a wonderful French restaurant which I think you will really like; you can tell us how authentic the food is."

"Oh, that sounds great. Incidentally, Mama says she has had a call from Brandon and he plans to be here the day before the rehearsal. Is that okay to include him?"

"Of course. I am really glad to do so for it is just right for the party to make it an even fourteen. Remind me to tell Mom when we get home."

"Okay. Who all is to be there?"

"Well, you and I, Mom and Dad, Eileen and Keith, Craig and Lynn Thornton, Mike Sanders, my Best Man, Maude, our Cook, your Mom and Brandon, George who, with Keith will Usher, and Karen who will be in charge of the Guest Book."

Oh, Rob, how nice of you to include Maude. I know plenty of people who would not.

"Maude is part of our family. She has been with us for about twelve years. I hardly remember when she wasn't with us."

Rob went into his Dad's den and made phone calls. One to the Café la Royale and to the Stafford Arms, a suite hotel, for reservations for Anne and Renee. He also made a reservation for Brandon Scott, as he requested, to be ready when Brandon arrived. He asked his Mom if she would call and invite the people for the rehearsal dinner and she promised to do so.

Janet had the invitation list ready, John Stewart had called and said the invitations would be ready the next morning. Rob picked them up as planned. Everyone was impressed with how pretty they looked. They were in pink, embossed in gold plate. The envelopes had gold inside the flap. "Oh, Mama, just look how pretty they look."

Mrs. Anne Darcel and Mr. and Mrs. Jim Farnsworth

Request the honor of your presence at the

Wedding and reception of their children,
Rob and Renee

On June 24, 1998
At six o'clock in the evening in
The garden at the Farnsworth home
1544 Meadowlake Place, Dallas, Texas

RSVP
809-341-9483

"Yes, my dear, they are perfectly beautiful."

Anne, Janet and Eileen had all volunteered to stuff envelopes and stamp them or even help address them, if necessary. Eileen offered to go to the post office and get the stamps. They spent the entire morning addressing and stamping envelopes. When Rob came home, he joined in and helped and by dinner time, they had them ready to mail the next morning.

"Whoever said the Farnsworths can't put together a wedding in just a few days doesn't know what they're talking about." said Jim with a chuckle, as they were finishing dinner that evening.

"That's a fact. It goes to show what teamwork can do."

"I am really tired. Does anyone mind if I go upstairs for a hot shower and an early night to bed?" asked Renee, with a yawn.

"Not at all. I am a little beat myself, Sweets," and Rob reached over and gave her a kiss goodnight.

"I think I will join her. I want to get my things together to move to the hotel tomorrow. I can't tell you, Jim and Janet, what a pleasure it has been to spend these few days in your lovely home. Thank you so much for your wonderful hospitality," Anne said, with a smile, as she and Janet cleared the table.

"It was our pleasure, Anne. We will be having you over for dinner every night if you will consent, and we will be doing several things together during the next week., I am sure." replied Janet.

"I heartily agree. We have enjoyed having you both and look forward to many times together," said Jim.

"That would be lovely to come for dinner. I am sure we will be spending quite a bit of time together anyway. Also, Rob, thank you, dear, for making the reservations for us and for Brandon. He will appreciate it too, I am sure. He is to call me tomorrow so I will tell him about it then."

Everyone said good night then and went off to their respective rooms for a good night's sleep.

Next morning, Maude had some sizzling bacon going and its aroma, together with that of freshly made coffee, drew almost everyone down to breakfast at once. "I have made Belgian waffles with hot butter pecan syrup or if you prefer, apricot jam."

"Smells wonderful. I could go for all of the above." Said Rob as he leaned over and gave Maude a hug.

'Well I knew you'd like it if I made waffles. Everyone get seated, I am halving them so that all of you can get started at once. They bake pretty fast, as you know."

When breakfast was over, Rob gave Renee a kiss goodbye ad left for the office. Jim said he had to go for a haircut and for a fitting for his tuxedo, so he would volunteer to take the invitations directly to the post office.

His offer was immediately accepted so Janet told Anne and Renee that she would drive them to the hotel, which was only a couple of miles downtown.

Just as they were leaving, Eileen called to talk with Renee. She told her that the shower was set for 7:30 the next night. Then she asked her to tell both their mothers and Maude that it would be at her house and that, of course, they were all to come.

Eileen told her that Lynn Thornton, Karen Busby, Katie Masters, Morgan White, Beth Sanders and a couple of her close friends who also knew Rob well would all be there. Morgan and Beth were, of course, wives of George and Mike who worked for Rob.

Janet drove them over and they got all settled. Then she went shopping to buy a couple of the items she knew Renee had selected on her Register., which she had gift wrapped. One was the set of every day dishes; the other the every day flat ware.

Meanwhile, Anne and Renee decided to walk down to one of the department stores where they went shopping. Anne had Renee select her spatulas, egg turner, wooden spoons, ladles, measuring cups and spoons, meat thermometer, marble rolling pin and dough board, a marble paper towel holder and a cheese slicer.

She bought a stainless steel coffee pot and toaster, as a wedding gift from Ria and Pierre, which Ria had asked that she buy for her. They had them all gift wrapped ready for the shower.

When they returned, there were two telephone messages, one from Rob and one from Brandon. Rob wanted to know if they'd be ready to be picked up for dinner at 5:30 so Renee called him right away to tell him okay. While he had her on the phone, he asked her to bring her swimsuit if she wanted to go swimming, which she did.

Anne took her call to Brandon and Renee went in to take a shower and freshen up before leaving for dinner, partly because she wanted to leave her mother alone to talk privately to Brandon.

They talked for a few minutes and Anne was smiling when she hung up. "Brandon said to say hello to you. He appreciated being asked to the rehearsal dinner and said he would be in on the day before. He said he would really like to invite the Farnsworths and the Clarks to have dinner with the three of us at the hotel dining room, the night he comes in on June 22."

"I think that would be lovely, Mama. I feel sure they would think so too. Are you about ready to go? Rob will be here in about fifteen minutes. Also, if you'd like to go swimming, take your suit as we are going to go in. Okay?"

"Yes, I am about ready. I just want to put on something else before we go. I don't think I will plan to swim, however."

Rob came and after a nice dinner, Anne and Janet played gin rummy while Jim watched TV. Rob and Renee had a great time swimming. Renee told Rob about Brandon's invitation and he thought it was really nice. Anne, in the meantime, told Janet and she said that they would love to do it. She said she'd have to check with Eileen and Keith, however, as they had a pretty busy social life.

When they got through playing cards, they talked about numerous things--their families, the wedding, the music and the invitations. "We should start getting responses very soon now. I have a card file set up to keep track of them which I devised for Eileen's wedding and it worked like a charm."

"Rob, could we plan to go to the department store tomorrow and make a final decision on our china silver, and crystal?"

"We definitely can and will. Right after lunch, we will do it. I promise. Incidentally, I just can't believe how smoothly everything has gone so far, can you? When I think of all of the things we have gotten done in three or four days, I get exhausted."

"Me too, it is as if I can't get enough rest."

"Well of course, you are in an entirely different climate than you are accustomed to and that definitely has a tendency to affect your energy level. I do apologize for running you so hard, Sweets, but I knew if we didn't get some things done first, we couldn't do the others and sometimes you just have to make a plan and work the plan to accomplish what you need to do. Anyway, we can pretty well relax for awhile now as everything that has to be done now has been done."

"I hadn't even thought of the climate change. You are probably right. I forgot to ask. Rob, do you and your attendants have to rent tuxedos?"

"Well, that brings up a good question. You know they have all sorts of colors in tuxedos and lots of people want to use them to go with their color scheme, particularly if they have a bunch of bridesmaids. Dad and I have black ones, but if you would like us to get colored ones, we will. The other guys will rent whatever color we say."

"Oh, I think black ones are fine. Eileen's dress is green and maybe a light green cummerbund with a green carnation boutonniere for each of you would look nice to carry out that color."

"That sounds good. I will tell the guys so they can be sure to go in for their fittings soon and not wait until the last minute. Renee, you look awfully tired, honey. Why don't I take you to the hotel so you can go to bed for a good night's sleep? We have been on the run so much, no wonder you are tired. Come to think of it, so am I. So we should both get some sleep."

"Okay, sounds good to me."

"I have a couple of meetings tomorrow morning and I need to take one of my new clients to lunch. I hope you don't mind my not being here to eat with you. I should be through about two and then we will do something. How about if we go to a movie matinee? I haven't done that for a very long time but I think it would be fun to do with you."

"The movie sounds great and no, I don't mind. I realize you have to work, Rob, and I also realize that the type of work you do requires you to take people to lunch sometime. It is perfectly all right, Sweetheart, so no need to apologize. I will take you up on your suggestion to take me home to bed. I have to admit, I am tired and the Jacuzzi after the swim just sapped all my strength. I feel kinda like a rag doll."

"You are a doll all right, but not a rag one. You are my sweet wonderful doll and I love you so much," he said with a hug and kiss. "Come on and let's go."

They walked into the living room where Anne and Janet were talking and announced that he was taking Renee to the hotel to go to bed. Anne said "that is a great idea. I am ready also. Thanks for a lovely evening, Janet. Thanks to you both for a wonderful dinner."

"It was our pleasure." chimed both Janet and Jim. "See you tomorrow. I think we'll have a backyard barbecue. How does that sound? We will call and ask Eileen and Keith if they'd come over too."

"Sounds great."

Renee gave both Jim and Janet hugs and said thanks and goodnight.

When Rob kissed Renee goodnight, she went into the sitting room, hugged her mom goodnight, then to her room and practically fell into her bed; she was asleep within minutes.

Both Anne and Renee slept in until about 9:00 o'clock. They got dressed and went down to a small café that served breakfast all day and had a leisurely meal.

"It feels kinda good just to relax a bit doesn't it, Mama?"

"Yes, it really does, my Cherub. You have been running so much I know you are very tired. I am very proud of you and Rob for the efficient way you have organized your time and gotten things done. I wouldn't have believed you could get this much done in so little time, but everything is practically ready for your wedding. Has Rob said where you will go on your honeymoon?"

"Yes, he has mentioned a cruise to Hawaii. I am very excited about it as I have heard so much about it, I am anxious to go there. Also, Mama, I meant to tell you, we are going to live in Rob's apartment for the next four months. After that, we will move into the new condos which are due to be completed then. We get to pick out all the colors, wallpaper, tile, draperies, flooring and cabinetry. Isn't that great? Rob says we will buy new furniture to go in it. It is all so exciting I can hardly believe it is happening to me."

"I know, my dear. I am so very happy for you. Rob's family is so wonderful too. I feel very confident about leaving you in his and their care. You are a very lucky young lady, but then, I think they are lucky getting you too."

"Thank you, Mama. I am a very lucky girl in another way, too. To have a great Mother like you." and she reached over and gave her Mom a big hug.

"Do you feel up to going shopping for awhile, Renee? I want to buy my dress for the wedding and I want you there with me. I saw one at Macy's that I liked very much, but I didn't try it on. I would also want to buy a hat, shoes and purse to go with it."

"Oh yes, Mama, let's do it. I would also like to buy some white capris and some new sandals as well as another bathing suit, especially since we are going to Hawaii."

So they went on a shopping spree and were lucky enough to find just what they wanted after shopping in two or three stores. They had all their packages sent to the hotel as they decided to walk back for the exercise. After walking in the Dallas heat for about thirty minutes, however, they were very hot and very tired. "Oh is it ever great to get inside this air conditioned building, I didn't think we would ever get here. Are you okay, Mama?"

"Yes, but, like you, I am very hot and exhausted. I am going to take a cool shower and then a short nap."

"I'm going to get my bathing suit on and go out to the pool for a swim, myself. Then I will come in and shower and get ready to go to the Farnsworths for the barbecue tonight,"

"Okay, dear, have a good swim but don't stay out too long or you might get a sunburn."

"Okay, Mama. I won't. See you later."

Renee swam for awhile and was very surprised to look up and see Rob standing around the pool. He came over and said "There you are. We had the same idea. I came home early and thought you'd like to go early to the folks' home and get in a swim before the barbecue."

"Oh Rob, I would have liked that. I am ready to get out so we can still do that. It is much shadier over there and I feel like I have had enough sun."

Rob helped her out and she slipped on the short robe and her thongs and they went up to her suite. Rob waited while she put on something to ride over in and took some other clothes to put on after the swim. "Mama was so tired, she is taking a nap. I really hate to awaken her."

"Then don't -- let's just leave her a note by the phone and have her call when she is ready to be picked up for the cookout. I will do it." He sat down and wrote the note. Renee came in ready to go.

"Hey, you, I'm glad you got home early. Do you realize I haven't seen you all day?" Renee said as she put her arms around him.

"I certainly do realize it. That's why I came home early. So, here is a good-morning kiss and then a I'm-going-to-work kiss and now a hello-darling-I'm-home-kiss!" and he hugged her tightly while smiling at her all the while.

"I could get used to this, Mr. Farnsworth" Renee said sweetly. I don't ever want it to end."

"I promise, it won't. I love you."

"I love you too, Rob. Oh, I can't wait for you to see my new stuff I bought. The store will deliver it tomorrow."

"Good, I'm glad you found some things you like. Speaking of tomorrow, honey, how about if we go do the Register thing as soon as the store opens tomorrow? I'm sorry we didn't do it today as planned but I just couldn't get away any sooner."

"That will be great to get that done."

I thought since we are going to Hawaii, it would be nice to have a couple of changes. I found two bathing suits I liked and couldn't decide which one to get so I bought them both. I found a couple of capri sets and another pair of white shorts, with a cute t-shirt to go with it. I also got a sun hat and I bought us matching beach towels. Mama bought the loveliest lilac linen outfit with shoes hat and bag to match for our wedding. She looks so great in it."

"She is a pretty lady anyway." Your clothes sound real cute, honey and I could really use a new beach towel--thanks. What color is my Mom going to wear or do you know?"

"She said she liked pastel blue and had already picked her outfit and accessories. Eileen has a pale green chiffon dress that is waltz length like my wedding dress and made very similar to it. It will work great."

"Well, everyone is all set with their tuxedos and I specified the pale green satin cummerbunds, with white ruffled shirts and green ties. The tuxedos will all be in black, except mine and I will wear white, which I have rented so I'll be like you." he said, as he smiled.

"That is great. I think white will be better. You should look different than the others."

"Well here we are, Sweets. Are you sure you want to go back in the pool since you've already swam over there?"

"Yes, I didn't have a handsome man to swim with over there. I will meet you at the pool in a few minutes. I need to say hi to Mom and Dad first."

"Me too. I came directly to the hotel from work so I haven't seen them either."

Janet and Jim were sitting in the den having a glass of cold lemonade when they entered the room. After greetings all around, Janet poured a nice tall glass for both of them. Then they got ready and went into the pool for a swim.

Soon, Eileen and Keith came and got into the pool too. They all had a lot of fun playing with the basketball and hoop and splashing each other and laughing when each other missed the goal. When they got out, they found that Anne had called and Jim had gone after her at the hotel.

"What can we do to help with the cookout, Mom? Would you like me to start the barbecue?" asked Rob.

"Yes, if you please, dear. Maude has made a large pot of baked beans, potato salad, green salad, and a large chocolate cake which we will have with homemade ice cream later. I also have the coffee pot ready to plug in if we decide we want some. We are having steaks on the barbecue and some of Maude's super yeast rolls."

"Oh, that sounds so good. What can I do to help?" asked Renee.

"Me too, Mom. Did Maude make banana nut ice cream?" asked Eileen.

"As a matter of fact, yes, she did, dear. You can both help.

"Now, let me see. Renee, take that large table cloth and put it on the big patio table. We will use the everyday flatware from that drawer on your right and the large paper napkins are in the drawer to your left. Allow at least two for each person as this kind of food can get messy.

Eileen, get the large ironstone plates and put them on. I have made lots of lemonade for which we will use the large plastic glasses so get the ice in them. Then, if you girls will finish setting the table by getting all the condiments on, that will be great."

As Renee began her task, she said to Janet, "Oh, I wanted to tell you that we did get the outfit Mom was talking about in lilac and it is very pretty. She was able to get beautiful accessories for it too."

"Oh, I am glad she found what she wanted, dear. I know she will look very pretty in that color."

"Mama just had to have a rest when we got home as we were both very tired and hot when we got through. We made the mistake of walking to the hotel instead of taking the street car or a taxi. We thought we needed the exercise, but I don't think we needed that much" Renee said, laughing.

"Oh my child. It is much too hot to walk very far during the summer here. You could get heat stroke. You didn't carry your packages, did you?"

"No, we had them sent to the hotel. They will come tomorrow."

"That's good. Oh, I think I hear Jim and Anne. Hi Anne, I hear you had quite a shopping trip today."

"Well yes, we did and it was successful but we got very warm walking to the hotel. I took a cool shower and had a nice long nap, which I desperately needed, so I am fine now. Give me a job so I can help you."

"Well, I think Jim and Rob have just put the steaks on so we could probably put the food on in a few minutes. Our homemade ice cream is done and packed in ice. The girls have the table all set. Why don't you have some lemonade and just sit here with me until they say we are about ready. There's also some chips and clam dip there. Help yourself."

"Sounds great. I had a call from Brandon and he is really looking forward to coming for the wedding. He will come on the twenty second."

"It will be nice to meet him. Oh, Anne, I wanted to mention to you that I plan to get my hair and nails done the day before the wedding. Would you and Renee like an appointment at the same time? It is a large shop so we could all go at once if that is okay with you two."

"Yes, I would like that, thank you. I am sure Renee will want one too. Let me ask her now." Anne stepped out on the patio where Rob, Jim and Renee to ask her. She came back in and said both Eileen and Renee would love to go to the beauty shop."

Soon the food was ready and everyone enjoyed the delicious meal. They sat around for awhile and talked.

Then Rob and Renee, Eileen and Keith decided to go for a drive. They drove around for awhile and then went up to a very popular view point and looked down at the lights of the city. They sat and talked, laughed, and made plans and then took Eileen and Keith back to their car at the house so they could go home.

Afterward, they sat in the car, did a fair bit of "cuddling" and then decided they had better go home. Then they went by the house, picked up Anne and went to the hotel. Rob walked to the door of the suite with them, said goodnight to Anne, kissed Renee and left.

Next morning, Renee was awakened by a knock at the door. She looked at the time and it was 8:45. She grabbed a robe and went to the door to see Rob all fresh in a short-sleeved polo shirt and walking shorts and sandals.

"Hello, sleepy head. Did I wake you up or are you just slow in getting dressed?"

"I'm sorry to say, I just woke up. Do we have time for me to shower real quick?"

"Of course. I just came on, thinking I would take you to breakfast before we go to the store to look at china, silverware, and crystal."

"Okay, you make yourself at home and I will get ready quickly. I will wear shorts and sandals too so we'll be a matched set."

"Sounds good to me, Sweets. We are a matched set already, as we go perfectly together." he said, grinning at her.

As Rob sat in the sitting room reading the paper he had brought in, Anne came in from her bedroom and greeted him. "Good morning. My we are late getting up and around today. How are you, Rob?"

"Just great. I came to take you all to breakfast as Renee and I have to go to the department store for the registry as soon as it opens."

"Rob, I think I will pass on going out to breakfast. Thanks, anyway. I will just go down to the coffee shop later when I get dressed. That way, I can take my time and you two can go ahead when you are ready and not have to bring me back."

"Okay Anne. If you want to go someplace before then, Mom said to call her."

"Okay, thank you, I will. Goodbye."

Renee hugged her Mom and said goodbye and they left for breakfast.

They talked while they ate about the wedding, the apartment, the planned honeymoon and all things that were important to them. They were both smiling as they left the restaurant and walked down, arm in arm, to the department store. They decided on Gorham for their sterling, Waterford for their crystal and Lennox for their china. Renee also took Rob around to see a lot of the things she chose on the Registry list.

"I think you did a great job, Sweetheart. Our tastes must be a lot alike as I am really very happy with your selections."

"Oh, I am so glad, Rob. Your Mom and Eileen have been helpful to me concerning some things you like, so I didn't do it all alone."

"While we are talking about 'tastes' I want us to go over to my apartment now and have you look at the curtains and see if you are comfortable with them. If you want to change the color or type they are, it is fine. We'll take whatever measurements we need. Afterwards, let's come back to the store and at least buy a new set of sheets, towels, and a new bedspread for our bed, and perhaps new curtains for the bedroom and kitchen. What do you think?"

"I'll be glad to go and look at everything with you, honey, but you know they are giving us a shower in two days. Why don't we do this: write down possible changes, if any, we want to make, but delay buying anything new until after the shower. Don't you think that makes sense?"

"Well, yes, of course it does, Sweets. However, I think we should go ahead and get new curtains for the kitchen and a bedspread and curtains for our bedroom, because no one is going to buy that for us, I don't think, do you?"

"I suppose you're right about that. In fact, I'm sure you are as that is something rather personal to the people using them day after day. Let's go and look and I promise if I really don't like your current decor, we will buy something else."

"Okay. It's a deal. But I do want to tell you that I had absolutely nothing to do with the decor I currently have so it won't hurt me in the least if you hate it."

Renee started to laugh and said, "Well I know I don't hate it. The best I remember is being impressed with how nice it looked, so I doubt that I would change much, if anything."

After they looked at the apartment, they decided together that some new curtains for the kitchen would be nice. The bedspread was a beautiful dark blue quilted satin and the draperies were the same blue satin with delicate white lace panels. Renee liked them very much and said she didn't want to change the bedroom.

They measured the windows in the kitchen and then went back to the store and bought some very pretty kitchen curtains made of yellow chintz with white organdy ruffles and tie backs. They also purchased a set of place mats with napkins to match and a set of dish towels.

"Now, I feel like we are getting ready for a home of our own, don't you?"

"Yes, and it feels so good. I can't wait until we are ready to really move in, or should I say until I am ready to move in?"

"Well, time is passing, my love, pretty fast when you consider all that has to take place yet. Tomorrow night is your shower at Eileen's and the next day, we will bring all of the gifts over here to the apartment. At that time, we can put up the new curtains in the kitchen. Okay?"

'That is a good plan. I can also bring clothes that I don't plan to take to Hawaii over here and put them away, as well as stuff Mama and Ria bought for us, can't I?"

"Yes, because Lois already has the closet and chest of drawers emptied out for you. We will choose a large dresser and chest for our new furniture that will be big enough for both our clothes in one room when we get to the condo. Also, remember we will have large walk-in closets.

Another thing, honey, I need to ask you. Remember that Lois asked if she could continue to clean for us after we got married? I told her I would let her know as we didn't really know for sure where we would live. Now that we know, do you want her to continue to come once a week and do the heavy cleaning?"

"I could do it myself after I get things organized. I will have plenty of time on my hands. Maybe we should continue to have her just once a week until we move to the condos."

"Well, you may be getting involved in other things and not have so much time on your hands, by then. Remember our discussion about the possibility of your going to school."

"Oh yes, I do remember that. You are going to teach me to drive first, I think, aren't you?"

"Yes, and while we are thinking of it, we are going to the DMV right now and pick up a copy of the driving rules for you to study in preparation for you to get your Learner's Permit. We have to be back as I think you ladies have a beauty shop appointment, right? Shall we have a quick lunch first?"

"Yes we do have an appointment and I do think it is a good idea to eat first as it will be quite a long time before we are through with the appointments at the Beauty Shop."

"After your beauty appointment, if it isn't too late and you still want to, we will go to the movie we didn't get to see the other day. We will grab a bite of dinner out, but we should tell Mom we won't be there to eat and if your Mom wants to go back to the hotel before we get back, Mom or Dad will take her."

"I would really like to do that."

"How about if we go have some Tex-Mex Mexican food? I'll bet you have never had anything like that."

"Well, no I haven't, but I am willing to try it."

They went back to the Farnsworth home and Renee joined her Mom, Janet and Eileen and went to the beauty salon for the 'works'. It was almost seven o'clock before they returned. Janet had warned Maude earlier that they would not be back until around then so she was to hold dinner until that time. She had put out snacks for Jim and Rob while they were waiting.

Rob and Renee went to the Mexican restaurant and she liked the food at once, except the very hot stuff. Then they went to the movie theater to see a very beautiful love story with Cary Grant and Deborah Kerr.

"Rob, do you realize that this is the first time we have ever been to the movies alone? Always before, Ria was with us."

"Yes, I do realize that and I hope that you will remember that they were good times too. But remember this first and foremost: you are first in my heart and always will be. Please try to forget what's past and think of all the times we have spent together as preparing us for today and forever. Will you please do that, my sweet?"

"Yes, I will try. But sometimes it is hard to forget the pains I had in my heart before I knew you loved me."

"I've always loved you, Sweetheart. I was just too dumb to realize that you were the one I visualized in my heart until I saw your picture. But that is all behind us now, so let's just go forward as of now. Okay?" and he squeezed her with the arm he had around the back of her seat.

"Okay, honey. I agree."

When the movie was over, they went back to the hotel and watched another movie with Rob's head in Renee's lap. She sat stroking his hair, and every now and then he would pull her head down and kiss her. They talked of their plans for the apartment, the honeymoon and many other things of interest to them.

When Anne came in, Rob said "well I guess I had better leave. I have to work until noon tomorrow." He turned to Renee and continued, "since your shower is tomorrow night, the guys are giving me a Bachelor party. It will probably be going later than the shower, if I know those guys, so you'd better plan to have Eileen drop you all off at the hotel."

"I'd like to suggest that it will be easier to unload your gifts at Mom's house than trying to get them up to the hotel at night.

Then we will pick them up the next day and take them all over to the apartment. What do you think?"

"I think that is a splendid idea, don't you Mama?"

"Yes, I do. We should stop by the house first so that we can help unload it."

The next night, Renee felt a bit shy walking into a roomful of strangers, but it didn't take long for her to feel right at home. Everyone was so friendly and welcoming and all seemed to hold the Farnsworths in such high regard that she felt very proud being a part of their family. Her mother joined right in with the group and won one of the prizes given for winning one of the games played.

The gifts were many, some very large and some small. She was given a beautiful white peignoir set and matching house shoes from her mother as a surprise gift in addition to all of the household goods she had already given her.

She got a coffee pot, a toaster, a blender, an electric mixer, an electric roaster, frying pan, a waffle iron and wok. She got a crepe maker, three blankets, a king-sized set of sheets, a cream-colored damask dinner table cloth with twelve matching napkins and numerous other items like a potato peeler, electric can opener, and a waffle iron. She also got the everyday dishes and flatware from Janet and Jim.

The shower party was fun and Renee felt that she made several very nice friends. All of them were invited to the wedding and had returned the card saying they would attend.

Renee made a mental note to check the list and see who had not yet responded. They had invited eighty and as of yesterday sixty-five had accepted the invitation. With eight of the family, including Brandon, that left only seven they had not heard from. They were supposed to give the Caterer notice of the exact number expected by tomorrow.

When the shower was over, Eileen drove to the Farnsworth home and with Jim's help, they brought all of the gifts and put them in the den to be picked up tomorrow. She then drove Anne and Renee to the hotel.

"Eileen, thank you so much for making it possible for me to have a nice shower. You have such nice friends. But most of all, I am glad you are my friend. I will look forward to having you as another sister. And I hope you will feel the same. I want you to feel free to ask me if you ever need anything I can do for you."

"It was my pleasure, Renee. I am looking forward to having a sister. Sometimes you need someone in the family close to your age although I am older than you. The same goes for me; feel free to ask me for help anytime."

"My, those friends of the Farnsworths were really generous to you and Rob, weren't they?" Anne said as they walked into their suite.

"Oh yes, Mama. Can you believe all of the nice things I have to start out with before we are even married? I am so pleased and grateful."

"I know you are, my Cherub, and I am so happy for you. Things just seem to be working out in all directions for you, don't they?"

"Yes they do. I am almost afraid, because things seem too perfect."

"Don't be afraid, dear, just enjoy each day and never fail to thank God for the wonderful blessings he has given you. Good night. I love you."

"I won't forget, Mama. I always try to tell God I am thankful for what he allows to happen to me. Goodnight, Mama. I love you too,"

The next day, Rob came to the hotel about one o'clock. He had stopped by and loaded all the gifts from his folks' house to move them to the apartment.

'Sorry, I couldn't get away sooner. I had a staff meeting at eleven and it ran over. I thought it would save time if I just stopped over and picked up the things first. Are you about ready to go?"

"Yes. I asked Mama to go over with us so she could see where we are going to live."

"Oh that's great, Anne. Do you all mind if we stop by and pick up some hamburgers and fries and take it to the apartment to eat? I have plenty of cold soda in my refrigerator."

'That is a good idea. I haven't had one of your American hamburgers before and I am anxious to try them."

"Neither have I and I would really like to try them, also. I want to see what you call 'French' fries, too,"

Renee said, with a grin.

They went to the apartment, took out some of the gifts they thought they might use right away when they returned from Hawaii and stored the rest in the spare closet. They also put away the things Renee and her Mom had bought plus some clothes she didn't intend to take on her honeymoon. They ate their hamburgers and fries first and both Renee and Anne said they enjoyed them immensely.

"I would imagine these would be quite popular in Paris don't you, Mama? I doubt if they would call the potatoes 'French'; they would likely call them 'American fries," she said laughingly.

When they returned to the Farnsworth home, Janet checked the invitation list and noted that four more had accepted. The three others who sent regrets, all from one family, had prior vacation plans but indicated that a gift was on its way.

So, Janet was able to call the Caterer and give an exact number who planned to attend the wedding and reception. When they called, Miss Lee, the Planner from the Caterer shop, asked that they come in and look over the favors that were to be placed at each place on the tables. They were pleased with them and to see that they were also in their chosen colors of pink and mint green.

For the favors, they had Jordan almonds in a little pocket, made of colored tulle lace tied with satin ribbon at the top, with silver letters spelling 'Renee and Rob' on the side of each one. The cocktail napkins also had the same theme with 'Renee and Rob, June 24, 1999. They also decided to have a whipped cream frosting on the white cake along with the lemon filling, with the decorations they had previously chosen. They also ordered a sherbet punch.

Now that all the invitations had been accepted and everything was all set with the Caterer, the Florist, and the Minister,

Jim asked if they would like to have him bring over the little orchestra and give them a sample of their music.

Everyone thought this a great idea so they quickly prepared a chip and dip, hot dogs and potato salad for a picnic on the patio. Maude had a plate of brownies and chocolate chip cookies for dessert, with plenty of cold drinks.

The guys were all jovial fellows who thoroughly enjoyed food and festivities, however small. They were all retired, neat, older men, whom the Farnsworths had known for years. Some had gone to college together and all were friends.

After they ate, they listened to Ben on the cello, Dave on the violin, Jerry on the flute, Bill on the sax, Joe on the bass fiddle with Sam at the drums. In all, everyone thoroughly enjoyed the music and the evening.

"Do you realize that Brandon will be here day after tomorrow? Don't forget, he has invited all of us to dinner that night." said Anne to Janet, with a smile.

"Yes that is right, isn't it? The time since you arrived here to now has really passed by quickly. I guess it is because we have filled each day to the brim. Know you will be glad to see Brandon. We are anxious to meet him. It is nice that he has asked us to dinner."

"Yes, I have to say I will. He loves to play bridge, Janet. Maybe you and Jim and he and I could have a game after dinner. I am sure the kids will all have someplace to go or something to do."

"What a great idea. Let's plan it. I am sure Jim would enjoy it too."

"Incidentally, Rob, Brandon asked if you would make reservations at a place of your choice for dinner that night. He will be in around 3:00 PM and will go straight to the hotel.

Of course, I will be glad to do so. Any idea what kind of food he particularly likes?"

"From what I have seen, he likes most anything. However, since we are in cattle country, why don't we try a nice steak house, if none of you have an objection."

I'm sure there will be no problem with the Texas bunch. How about you, Sweetheart?"

"That's sounds fine to me too."

"Well, I think I am ready to go to the hotel for the night if you all are ready to take me. Thanks so much for a lovely evening. The food and entertainment were just wonderful."

"I'm ready to go too, Rob. I also say thank you to all the musicians. It was delightful."

"Thanks also for your never-ending hospitality and great food, Mom and Dad," said Renee, after giving them both a hug.

"It is our pleasure to have you both. Goodnight all."

After saying good night, Renee went in cleaned her face, brushed her teeth and went to bed. She had trouble going to sleep, however, as she felt very uncomfortable as her stomach began to ache and she thought maybe she had eaten too much. The pain persisted and seemed to get worse even though she took some anti-acid tablets.

After some time without any improvement, she decided she had better go in and tell her Mother, who was already asleep by this time. She woke up and got out of bed as Renee entered her room as she could tell that something was wrong. She felt of Renee's forehead, which was very hot. She said she had been in pain for several hours and had begun to have more pain. It seemed to be concentrated on her right side.

Anne called down to the desk clerk to see if they had a house Physician, which they did not. She then called Rob to tell him that Renee needed a doctor so he said he would be right over. "Just put a robe and shoes on her and have her ready to go to

Emergency Hospital. I will be as quick as possible." He was there in a very few minutes, came in and picked her up in his arms and took her down in the elevator to the car which was waiting by the door.

A little while later, they were in Emergency, Anne was filling out necessary information, while Rob was in with the Dr. who was talking with her. He said that based on her symptoms, he was sure it was her appendix so he put in a call to the on-call Surgeon to come in immediately.

She was admitted and prepped for surgery as soon as possible for the Surgeon said it was an emergency to prevent a rupture. After the surgery, he said she came through just fine, but that it was a good thing she came when she did or she might not have made it. Rob and Anne both cried and hugged each other at the relief they felt at her recovery from such a close call. They were so thankful to God that she was okay.

The nurse came out after several hours which seemed like days to both of them, and told them they could come in one at a time. Rob insisted that Anne go in first. "Tell her I will be in next."

"Thank you., Rob, I appreciate your consideration. I won't stay long for I know you are anxious."

Anne went in and saw her youngest daughter, lying there pale and half asleep. She went up to her, kissed her and told her how much she loved her.

"Oh, Mama, I knew everything was too perfect. Now this had to happen. What can we do about the wedding?"

"Renee, my Cherub, don't fret about that right now. You have been through a serious ordeal. You must concentrate on getting well. That is the important thing right now. Rob is very anxious about you and wanting to come in, so I will leave now and see you later. Okay?"

"All right, Mama."

Rob came in and took her hand and kissed it and then leaned over and kissed her. "Oh, my darling, I have been so worried about you. I am so thankful that you are going to be okay."

"But Rob, what about our wedding? This just ruins everything. I just knew something would happen as everything has been so perfect up to now. What can we do?"

"Don't you worry about a thing. The only thing we have to postpone is going on our honeymoon trip, but we will do that just as soon as you are able. I promise. I will call them today and leave our departure date open."

"But you know I can't walk down the aisle and stand up for a wedding ceremony. Our rehearsal is day after tomorrow and the wedding is supposed to be the day after."

"That is true, Sweetheart. I promise you we will get married on that day if it has to be here in the hospital."

"Oh but I so wanted it to be in the garden. What will happen to all our plans? Is it not too late to cancel all of that?"

"I will just have to see what can be done or if I can postpone it for a later date. If we can, we will use it for the reception and sit-down dinner when you are able. I believe I can, if I do it today. I will go right away and talk to the Caterer, then I will call the Florist."

"Oh, Rob I am so sorry I messed things up" Renee said, with tears streaming down her face.

"Now you just stop that. You didn't do anything to mess things up. You couldn't help getting sick and you know it." He took her in his arms and hugged her. "There's no use crying about things that can't be helped and I am going to try and see if they can. Just remember, darling, 'it is not what happens to you that matters--what does matter is your reaction to what happens."

"My reaction now is utter disappointment. I hate to disappoint everyone who was coming to our wedding. It was going to be such a beautiful event and now I have just ruined it." Renee cried as if her heart would break. Rob did his best to console her, but it was next to impossible. She couldn't accept it.

Then she said. "Rob, honey, you go ahead and do what you need to do. I will be okay. I know you are right about accepting things over which you have no control, but it is so hard. Will you come back as soon as you can? I want you with me, please."

"Yes, my darling, I will be back as soon as possible. You try and get some rest and please don't cry any more. It doesn't help you at all to get well when you are so upset. You need to think positive. I am leaving now and will see you soon." He said after he kissed her goodbye.

One by one, Jim, Janet, and Eileen went in to see her and encourage her, after which her Mom went in again. Soon, a nurse came in and moved her bed into a room where she was to stay while in the hospital. The nurse gave her some pain medicine and said "she will probably sleep the whole afternoon, so why don't you go home and get some rest yourself? I will call if she asks for you or if there is any change in her condition."

So they all left to go home. They took Anne by the hotel so she could go to bed for awhile. She had a good long nap, got up and showered and dressed as Brandon was due in about 3:30.

She was so distressed because Renee was so sad, and was going to miss the festivities that had been planned. Rob was going to do his best to make things work out even if different from the original plans. He was such a wonderful young man. If she had picked someone as her own son, she couldn't have done better than Rob. And he would make Renee happy. There was no doubt about that.

Rob decided to try something different than what he had suggested to Renee. He asked to talk to the Surgeon before he left the Hospital. He told him they were to be married in two days and asked if it would be possible for her to be released by that time to go to his parents' home. The Dr. said he saw no reason why not, if she was doing okay by that time. Rob asked if he could rent a hospital bed and a wheel chair for a couple of days. The Dr. said that would not be a problem.

Afterward, Rob called an ambulance service and arranged for Renee to be picked up at noon on her wedding day, June 24. They had planned to be married at 6:00 PM and he was determined it was going to happen if she was in a wheel chair or even a hospital bed!

He called the Caterer, who said they could make a few adjustments by making the arch wide enough for a wheel chair or hospital bed. He left all other arrangements intact, except changing the number for dinner reservations that night. He decided to have dinner at the hospital with Renee instead of at the Steak House, as planned, with Brandon.

When he arrived back at the hospital, after grabbing a bite of lunch, he called his office to let them know what had happened and also Craig and Lynn. His Mom decided to call a few of their closest friends to tell them all about Renee. The news spread quickly and most of those invited were aware that things would be a little different than planned, but that it would still happen.

Meanwhile, about 3 o'clock, there was a knock on the door of Anne's hotel suite. She answered and to her surprise, it was Brandon who took her in his arms and kissed her. She was a bit taken aback but smiled and said "I didn't expect you so soon. I thought it would take longer for you to get here from the airport."

"Well, I had called ahead and made reservations for the car and they had it waiting for me. I just had a hang-up bag and a carry on so I didn't have to check luggage. That saved me a wait and in addition to all that, we arrived fifteen minutes early."

"That is wonderful. I am so glad you are here for I have so much to tell you."

Then she told him all about Renee and also where they were to have dinner. She told him Rob wanted to stay with Renee for dinner so there would just be the six of them.

"So, what about the wedding? Will they still be able to get married?"

"I don't really know. Rob says yes. I don't know how. I only know that Rob said he would work it out and if I know Rob, that is exactly what will happen. I haven't seen him or talked to him since we left the hospital so I have no idea what he is cooking up."

Anne called room service and ordered some sandwiches and iced tea. So for the next two or three hours, they visited and talked to each other about what all had been happening in their lives since they had seen each other. Brandon said he was thrilled to be invited to the wedding so he could see her again before she left for France and was doubly thrilled she had agreed to go early to New York and spend a few days with the Browns and him.

I have missed you, sweet lady, and I can't tell you how much time I have spent thinking of you and counting the days until I would see you again. It is almost scary to me, Anne, as I haven't had these feelings for a long time."

"I have missed you too, Brandon and have been looking forward to your coming. Incidentally, would you like to play bridge after dinner? Janet and Jim have invited us over to play, if you would. I do want to go to the hospital to see Renee before we go to dinner. Is that okay with you? I know she would like to see you, too."

I would love to see Renee. I would also like to play bridge. Why don't we go to the hospital now?"

They went to the hospital and Renee was just waking up a bit. She wasn't feeling too good as the anesthetic had made her nauseous and the nurse had just given her medication for it.

She smiled weakly at Brandon when he spoke to her and told him she was glad he had made it. They talked a bit and then Rob came in, smiling, with a big bouquet of roses for her. There was another bouquet of flowers on the side table from Janet and Jim.

Rob leaned over and kissed her and brushed her hair away from her face. He asked her how she was feeling and she told him the problems she'd been having but she felt some better now. He told her he was having dinner with her so she's better have something good if he was going to eat there instead of going to the Steak House. He smiled and she knew he was back to his old teasing self.

He said" How would you like to know that we are going to get married, as planned, in the garden, as planned, except that, instead of walking, you get to ride down the aisle?"

"Oh Rob, do you really think we can do that? Will the Doctor let me out of here that soon?"

"I have already talked to him. He said if you continued to progress as you have, he sees no reason not to let you go home as long as there is someone to take care of you. He also says it won't hurt you to sit in the wheel chair if it isn't too long. We will take a hospital bed out to the tent to put you in if you get too tired. I have already made arrangements to have the bed, the wheel chair, and you taken to the house at noon on our wedding day. How does that sound?"

"That's sounds terrific. I was so afraid we couldn't work it out, but I should have known you would think of something. You are a genius and so sweet and wonderful."

"Thank you, sweetheart, I am glad you think so. Just call me 'persistent.' Now you must do your part by behaving yourself and doing everything you are supposed to do so you will be able to do that, okay? I am told you will be up and walking around a bit tonight. I will be here to walk with you."

"That will make it much easier if you are here with me."

Anne turned to Rob and said, "I, too, am so glad you worked things out, Rob. I know how much it means to you both. It may be slightly different going down the aisle, but most everything else can be the same. Just think of people who are permanently disabled and live in wheel chairs in otherwise normal lives. At least, yours will be only temporary," she continued as she looked at Renee.

"You are absolutely right. We have to learn to make lemonade out of lemons, my Mom always says" Rob answered, with a smile.

"And she is certainly right about that. I guess we had better be going so that we can go to eat with Janet and Jim. Janet suggested we come over and go with them. We will be playing bridge afterward, so we won't be back tonight. Is that okay with you Renee?"

"Of course, Mama. You all have a good time. I wish we could be going with you."

"I wish that too, sweetheart, but there will be other times. Goodnight. See you tomorrow."

The hospital had room service so one could order from the menu and it was brought to the room whether or not you were a patient. So, Rob was able to order a stuffed pork chop, cranberry sauce, creamed peas and a piece of chocolate cake with a cup of coffee. Renee could also order but hers was from the soft diet section, so she didn't fare so well. She had to settle for cream of chicken soup, apple sauce and milk. It was all she felt like eating anyway.

The next day was the day of the wedding rehearsal. Rob decided that it should go on as usual except that Lynn Thornton would stand in for Renee while the rehearsal was being held. Jim was elected to push the wheel chair with Anne walking beside it to give the bride away.

Renee insisted that Rob should attend the rehearsal dinner, even though she could not and he finally agreed. All went well and everyone enjoyed the dinner. The family all came up to the hospital for a quick visit to Renee before visiting hours were over. Rob stayed as long as he could, kissed Renee goodnight and told her to be ready to leave tomorrow about noon as the ambulance would be there to get her.

"Will you be with them?"

"Yes, I will."

"But Rob, I happened to think. You aren't supposed to see the bride on the wedding day until the ceremony."

"Sweetheart, we are going to have what is called a non-traditional wedding. We are going to lay aside all superstitions and just enjoy the day. So what? I will see you before the wedding. We know that will not cause bad luck. We are the luckiest people in the world already, because we have each other. So let's not worry about petty things, okay?"

"Okay, Rob, you are absolutely right. It is just a tradition, I know and no one has ever proved it did harm, as far as I know. We are going to just ignore it and do what we want to. Besides that, I think superstitions are pagan traditions and Christians aren't pagans."

"Now you're talking, Sweets. It's our party and we'll do what we want to." he said as he smiled and winked at her in his own inimitable way. "Now let's take that walk we're supposed to and then I am going to tell you goodnight for I want you to have a good rest. We have a big day tomorrow."

After Rob escorted her up and down the hall, IVs and all. They walked awhile and he could see she was getting tired and very ready to get back into bed. She was, however, at least smiling again.

"I am getting excited all over again. I have felt so rotten the last two days that I have hardly thought of anything else."

"I know you have, honey. You get a good night's rest now, and I will see you tomorrow."

"Goodnight. I love you."

"Goodnight, I love you too."

After Renee got her night medicine, she fell asleep and slept the entire night except for the times the nurse had to come in and take her vitals and see that she was okay.

When morning came, the nurse brought her breakfast, then the Doctor came in to see her. He told her he felt she was doing fine and said, teasingly, that he thought she would get much worse if he kept her in the hospital away from her wedding. Another nurse came in to bathe her, change her bed and help her into her own gown and robe. They kept her so busy she didn't have time to get anxious for Rob to come.

The first thing she knew it was already 11:00 AM and the phone rang. It was Rob saying good morning to her and telling her that today was her very last day to be known as Miss Darcel. He said he wanted her to know that he was very excited and considered himself very lucky that she was to become his bride this very day. She told him she felt very lucky too and couldn't wait to be called Mrs. Rob Farnsworth. He told her he would see her in a very little while.

Rob had come into the Business Office earlier to take care of all the paper work necessary to discharge her so that there would be no delay in transporting her to the Farnsworth home as soon as they arrived.

Janet had made up a downstairs bedroom and by the time Renee got there, she was ready to lie down for awhile. Janet made a light appetizing lunch for her with a cup of hot tea. Jim came in to see her for a few minutes and kissed her on the cheek.

"Your Mom called to see if you were here yet just before you arrived. I told her I would have you give her a call when you get all settled down. There's a phone by your bed when you want to do so."

'Thanks, Dad. I will give her a call."

"Thanks to you, Mom, for the nice lunch and for the comfortable bed. It sure feels a lot better than that hospital bed."

'It is my pleasure, dear."

Rob and Jim walked in and Rob told her they were going to go and pick up their tuxedos and would be back in a short while.

Janet came back in and sat down to talk with Renee and said, "You know I just happened to think of something. Why don't we schedule a special photo session with all of the wedding party when you are able to be up and around? I had already asked a good friend of ours who does weddings to do your pictures for you as one of your wedding presents. She can take pictures of all the decorations and the cake and the wedding as it goes on, but you might like to have a few with you standing with Rob and your wedding party also. What do you think?"

"I would like that. If I can possibly get into my dress, I might be able to stand for a couple or three minutes with Rob, at least. Do you think I could possibly wear it over this bandage?"

"Well, we can certainly give it a try. If it is too uncomfortable, I am going to suggest that you wear the white peignoir outfit with your veil, because if you are seated, no one can really tell much about what you have on. Then, in the later photos, they will get to see you in your pretty dress."

"I am going to call Mama now. Is it okay if she and Brandon come over? I will tell Mama to bring all of my stuff for the wedding including my going away bag with the peignoir set in it."

"By all means, have them come on over. If they haven't had lunch, tell them we have loads of stuff for sandwiches."

Brandon and Anne had been having a great time catching up with what each other had been doing. They'd really enjoyed the rehearsal dinner last night and the bridge game afterward with Janet and Jim.

She was so glad that she'd gotten well acquainted with Eileen and Keith too, especially Eileen. She was very impressed with her and felt happy that Renee would have her for a sister-in-law. She knew she would need a girl friend, especially since she would be missing Ria and her and her friends back home. After all, she had never even been away from her more than two weeks at one time in her entire life, so she was very likely to suffer some homesickness.

Janet and Jim were such wonderful people that they would do their best to keep her from being too lonely. She and Rob would be together a lot even after he went back to work so maybe she wouldn't miss them too much. However, that didn't help her much. She was going to miss her family as a whole so much and especially Renee who would be so far away. Tears came into her eyes as she hung up the phone and Brandon walked over and hugged her and wiped her eyes. "I know how you feel, Anne. It is hard to say good bye to your child no matter how old they are."

As she was getting Renee's gown and veil and shoes along with her overnight bag, tears suddenly came into her eyes again as she began to think of Renee getting married tonight. She thought, with a sinking feeling, "I am going to go off and leave my baby in a whole new country. How am I going to cope with her being gone so far away from me? I must not, in any way, let her know that as happy as I am for her, I am so sad to leave her and not live close to her any more. I am going to miss her so much. I will miss Ria being at home too, but, at least, I will see her and can pick up the telephone and call her often. All of a sudden, it isn't just one being gone. I will just miss 'us' as a family." At that, she just sat down and sobbed. Then when she had sat for a few minutes, she washed her face and replenished her make up before going back out.

When she went back into the living room where Brandon was waiting for her, he noticed that her eyes were a little red and being a very sensitive and caring person, he walked over and put his arm around her and asked, "what is the trouble, Anne? As if I didn't know."

"Oh Brandon, it has just hit me all of a sudden that I am losing my baby and I am going so far away from her. I just couldn't be happier for her marrying Rob. He and his family are so great, I know she will be taken care of, but I am just sad right now and I have to get it out of my system."

"I know, my dear. Connie and I had to go through those feelings, too. It just hurts to empty the nest. While our son and daughter are not in a different country, it feels almost like it at times, because they are not in my daily life any more and it does hurt, especially now since there are grandchildren involved. It is perfectly natural for you to feel that way. So, if you want to cry a few tears, just go ahead for I certainly understand it," and he gave her a hug and kissed her on her cheek.

"Thank you, Brandon. I needed that and I so appreciate your understanding. I will be all right now. I need to go freshen my makeup."

When she returned, Brandon said, "I want to tell you that you certainly make a beautiful mother-of-the-bride. I love that lilac outfit on you."

"Thank you, kind sir. You look very handsome also in that dark blue suit."

"Thank you. Shall we go?"

By the time Brandon and Anne arrived, Eileen and Keith, those of Rob's staff who were in the wedding, and the Minister and his wife were in the large living room.

Outside, the garden was beautifully decorated with flowers and the wedding archway set up. The large dining tent was set up and the musicians were getting their instruments in the corner where they would play. Rob and Janet went out to check to see that everything was going according to plan. The wedding cake was now mounted with the miniature bride and groom perched on top. The places were set. Outside a refrigerated truck held the food for the wedding feast.

Anne went into the room with Renee who was sitting on the side of her bed. Renee mentioned her and Janet's conversation that she would wear the peignoir if she couldn't wear the dress and Anne thought it a great idea. She removed her gown and slipped the slip over her head. So far, so good. When she put her dress on, Renee had to stand to pull it down. The dress had fit her perfectly and she didn't really think she could fit it over the bandage; however, she had lost weight while so ill and it zipped right over the bandage and didn't even show since the slip covered it.

Her Mom put her hose and peau-de-soie satin pumps on for her and then brushed her long dark brown hair which being naturally curly, looked beautiful as usual. She used only a speck of powder on her nose and a little bit of lipstick and she was ready. She needed no eye makeup as she had very nice natural eyebrows and thick, dark eyelashes framing her warm blue-gray eyes.

"Oh, Mama. Will you put my veil on now, so I can see how I look ?"

"You look absolutely beautiful. I have never ever seen a more beautiful bride."

"Oh, thank you, Mama".

Jim and Brandon knocked at the door and Anne answered it. Jim said, "Your chariot is ready, your highness, and we are your coachmen designated to carry you to your wedding. You look absolutely fetching, my dear and that is Texan for gorgeous."

Renee began to smile and they put her in the chair and rolled her out on to the patio and down a ramp they had set up on the side of the stairway, to the sidewalk and out into the garden.

When Renee saw Rob in his white tuxedo, she gasped with delight as did he when he saw her in her wedding dress. As the music began to play, Jim pushed the chair and her Mother walked alongside on her right side with Eileen on her left. The Best Man was already standing with the Minister and Rob. The rest, including Jim wore black tuxedos. Renee and Rob both had big beautiful smiles when they looked at each other.

The vows were meaningful and the music was moving and beautiful; they exchanged their rings and kisses and Rob pushed her back down the aisle and then back into the tent. Everyone exclaimed happily over the food and drinks and the cake. A large table of gifts was over to one side.

Everyone wished the happy couple well and were particularly pleased that Renee was able to attend her own wedding. It was something she and Rob would never forget. The food was delicious, the music beautiful, and the flowers were gorgeous. In all, it was a very successful party and a memory maker for all involved.

They left and went to Rob's apartment which was all fresh and spotlessly clean, thanks to Lois, and Renee was ready to lie down as she was very tired after being up for so long. Rob helped her get undressed and ready for bed as, of course, she couldn't do it herself, yet.

"We are going to laugh about this turn of events some day, my darling, as I am not going to be able to make love to you the way I want to, but that doesn't mean I can't sleep with you and hold you in my arms and love you. I can also wake up in the morning and see your sunny face."

"Oh, Rob, you are such a great sport about everything. The Doctor says I will be fine to go on our honeymoon in three weeks."

"In the meantime, we will keep ourselves busy doing some of the things we want to do such as pick out our decorations for our new condo and I will bring some brochures on furniture that we will look at too.

We need to open our wedding gifts, so I will take you back over to the folks' house tomorrow night to open them. Your Mom and Brandon have agreed to stay one more day so they can be there for that."

"Oh, that is nice. I had almost forgotten about the wedding presents and I do want Mama to be able to see them too."

"Before I forget, Renee, I have asked Lois to come in and clean and fix the meals for us until you are able to be up and around. She will continue to clean, but when you feel like it, we will just eat out until you are ready to show me what a good cook you are," he said with a grin.

"Oh, that will be nice. I was getting worried about how I would manage, but I should have known you would have worked it out. You are spoiling me already. But you just wait, I will show you I'm a good cook and I will spoil you too!"

"I'm counting on it."

The next morning, Renee awoke to Rob bringing her breakfast in bed. There was crisp bacon, scrambled eggs and buttered toast, along with freshly-squeezed orange juice and hot coffee. He had cooked it himself, which made it even more special. He explained that he had asked Lois to start tomorrow as he wanted no company on their wedding breakfast. He moved a card table up close to the bed so he could eat with her.

They spent a wonderful day together, laughing and talking and planning. Rob put up the new kitchen curtains and put out their new His and Hers towels in their bathroom. Rob asked her what she would like for lunch and she said "pizza" so he ordered one with salad and they had lunch. They took a nap together afterward and about 5:00 in the evening, they were ready to go to the Farnsworth's for dinner and opening of their wedding gifts.

Anne and Brandon, Eileen and Keith were already there and they all sat down to dinner. Janet and Jim gave them service for eight of their sterling. Eileen and Keith gave them eight of their Waterford crystal water glasses, Brandon gave them a check for $250, her mother gave them a check for $250 in addition to all of the other gifts she had already bought.

They got several gift certificates from large department stores totaling $1,000. They got place mat and napkin sets, table cloth and napkin sets., a Waterford crystal salt and pepper, cream and sugar set.

They got a beautiful set of Farberware stainless steel cookware, three mixing bowls.,two cookbooks, and a starter set of six place settings of their Lennox china pattern. They got a stainless steel fryer, and a large roaster. They also got a round leather card table and four leather padded chairs. Renee was overwhelmed at all of the wonderful generous gifts of Rob's friends.

She and her mother had a few minutes alone before the evening was over and had a few tearful moments to say goodby as she and Brandon were leaving early on the plane to New York and Renee would not be able to go to see them off.

Rob and Jim had agreed to take them to the airport at 7:00 AM the next day. She agreed to take pictures of the condo when it was all decorated and had their new furniture all placed in it, so her Mom and Ria could see it. Rob had a very nice digital camera and camcorder and would be able to take some great pictures with it.

"If it is all right with you, Mom and Dad, could we just leave most of the gifts here until we move into our condo?"

Absolutely all right," said Janet. "We aren't expecting any company the rest of the summer and even if we do, we have three other bedrooms to use. Feel free to leave it as long as you need to."

"We have been given an approximate move-in date of September 15, which is only a month and one half instead of when I originally thought it would be. Of course, that is approximate. Even if it is Oct. 1, that would be good. It will be nice to be all settled by Thanksgiving. I thought you would like to know that we will be having Lois help us out with cooking and daily cleaning for the next three weeks. After that, we will be going on our Hawaiian Honeymoon Cruise for two weeks."

Oh, that is wonderful that you won't have so long to wait to get into the Condo. It is great too, that you can schedule your Cruise that soon. Lois is a nice person and she will be a great deal of help to you."

The next day Jim and Rob dropped Anne and Brandon off at the airport. Once they were settled in the plane, it wasn't long until they were in the sky. Brandon said "Anne this is so exciting to be taking a trip with you. I hope you won't think I am rushing things, but I don't want this trip to be the last we will see of each other. I am very attracted to you, as you have probably already guessed," he said as he reached over and squeezed her hand.

I hope it won't be the last we see of each other either, Brandon. We can keep in touch by phone and letters, and even e-mail. I want you to know that I feel very comfortable with you and I like you very much," she said smiling up at him.

"I like you very much too, Anne. If anyone had told me a month ago that I would meet someone I could really care for, I would not have believed them. I loved my wife very much and was always faithful to her. She told me once that if she preceded me in death, it would be a compliment to her for me to want to be married again. She said if we had not been happy, then she wouldn't expect me to want to be in that situation again. At the time, it didn't make sense to me, but it does now. Do you know what she meant?"

"Yes. I do. Bill and I felt the same way. We couldn't imagine not being married because we felt it was the only way to really live and be happy. I miss him terribly too as we were very much in love."

"Does that mean you think you could marry again?"

"Oh, I probably could some day, after a time, if the right person should come along."

Just as he started to make another comment, the Flight Attendant came with their refreshment snacks so he said, "Let's talk more on this subject when we can have a little privacy--maybe during our stay in New York City, and he smiled and reached over and squeezed her hand."

Meanwhile, back with the honeymooners, Rob and Renee were busily thinking of things they could do when they actually wanted to do something else. They eagerly looked at the brochures from the Condominium Complex and chose their colors, tile, flooring, wall coverings, window coverings, carpet, and cabinetry.

"We'll go over tomorrow and turn over our selections to the Sales person. Then we will select the lot and the model of apartment that we want. Then we will go out for a nice dinner. Let's see, we have had Chinese, Mexican, and American. Could you go for Italian?"

"Sounds good to me. I am getting my appetite back and if I keep this up, I really am going to have to go on that diet. I like Italian food."

"You know, Rob, I just thought of something we really need to get done and this is a great time to do it. We should take out time to write our thank-you notes for our wedding and shower gifts."

"That is a super idea and it is really important. Then it will all be done and we can forget about it. I know something else that I think is extremely important and that is for you to study your driving manual so we can get you a Learner's Permit. Then we can start your driving lessons. I want to buy your car so that you can learn on the one you will be driving. It will be much easier for you to gain confidence that way."

"I am so excited about that but I am a little scared too."

"You will get over that once you get a little experience. It is fun to drive. You wait and see. I honestly think you will love it and the freedom it affords you. You can shop or go other places as you wish when you can drive and have a car."

"Oh, I know it will be wonderful."

As they were eating, they also decided that next week would be a good time to go and look at furniture. Although Rob knew that Renee should not be on her feet too much until she was fully recovered, she seemed to be getting stronger and determined to rush getting well. It actually seemed to be working. He was insisting that she rest some every so often . . . especially since he was needing to be at the office part of the time. He wanted to be able to take off the full two weeks when they were able to go to Hawaii for their real honeymoon.

"You know you have to go the Doctor in a couple of days. I hope he will think I have taken care of you properly, but I doubt it, for you are a hard one to hold down."

"He will think you did a good job and will see I am fine. I feel as if I am almost well now. Oh, I want to be so badly!"

"I know you do, Sweets and you will." During the next week, they carried out most of their plans except for scheduling time for the driving manual. They did, however, go to a large furniture store where Rob's family had shopped for years because of its quality and variety of selection. Jim knew the owner, Joe Wright, quite well as they were in Rotary Club together. Joe had always been very fair and very helpful.

They selected French Provincial furniture in white ash, with gold trim. The coffee table, lamp tables and bedroom night stands had marble inlay tops. They selected two identical loveseats, upholstered in powder blue velveteen, two wing-back chairs done in light and dark blue striped satin material for the living room. They chose white and brass lamps with crystal prisms for the end tables and a large brass floor lamp. The carpeting was to be dark blue Berber.

The dining room would have an oval table with three leaves, six chairs, a lighted china cabinet and buffet. Custom covers would also be there for the table and leaves. The floor would be hardwood with a Persian area rug. The kitchen would have black Corian for the cabinet tops and the center island which would also be used as a breakfast bar. They chose four black leather bar stools with padded arms and backs. The floor tile would be white and black. Kitchen cabinets would be all white and appliances -- range, microwave, dishwasher and refrigerator would be black. There would be roll-out cabinets, a built-in spice drawer and an ample pantry.

Two bathrooms would have Corian vanity tops with white and black tile floors in various patterns. The Master bathroom would have a large bathtub with a Jacuzzi, and a separate shower. The double vanity would be Black Corian with white appliances.

"Oh Rob, can we really afford all of this? This just overwhelms me, thinking how much this will cost. I have never been able to go and pick out just anything I wanted."

Yes, we can, as a matter of fact. The furniture is a gift from my folks. When each of us decided to get married, my folks gave both me and Eileen a check for $20,000, specifically for buying our furniture without going into debt for it."

"How wonderful of them to do that. They are such great people and I am so lucky to be a part of their family."

"They love you too. And also, you need to know that, we are not without funds of our own. I have a pretty substantial checking and savings account. I intend to sit down with you soon and go over all of our assets and obligations for which we are responsible to pay each month. I want you to know what we have and to learn how to take care of them, if need be."

"I really would like to learn to do that. I am sure taking care of household bills would be a help to you. You have enough of that kind of work at the office."

"You are right and I will appreciate it. Now, let's saunter over to the bedroom stuff. Let's look again at the things we decided on, a king-sized bed with two night stands and lamps. I like this large double dresser with six drawers on each side and this six drawer chest. We also have a large flat TV to be put on a rack above the chest of drawers so both of us can easily see it."

"I like them all too. I guess we will have plenty of room for everything. I also like the pale blue ginger bowl lamps with the white satin pleated shades."

"Don't forget that we will have a walk-in closet in the dressing room off our bedroom and a linen closet in the hall next to the closet for guest wraps. That should give us a lot of room for all of our clothes and shoes and whatever else we want in there, like golf clubs." He said with a grin.

Joe Wright joined them and congratulated them on their marriage. He said, "Rob, I took the liberty of looking at your order and noticed that you have selected almost everything we had in the dining room display group except the Queen Anne crystal chandelier."

"Well yes, it is perfectly beautiful and I think we do need that. What do you think, Renee?"

"That crystal chandelier is just the most beautiful thing I have ever seen."

"Great. I am glad that you want it for I want to give it to you as a wedding present as well as in appreciation for your business."

"What a generous gift. Many thanks, Joe. It is very lovely and we are pleased with all of our other purchases too."

"Oh yes, we certainly are pleased and thank you so much."

"Just remember folks, if everything is not exactly as you want it when it is delivered, do not hesitate to call and we will make it right or my name isn't 'Wright,' he said as he smiled broadly at them."

"I appreciate that and know it to be true. We now need to shop for bedroom furniture for our guest room. What would you put in it, honey?"

"I think we should get a queen-sized bed, and maybe the same six-drawer double dresser with mirror. Let's also get a luggage rack that folds up. Since it also has a walk-in closet, it will be great for storing out-of-season clothes and extra pillows and such things."

"I agree. Since we will be getting the same furniture, how about getting the same night stands and lamps?" We can have different draperies with the same colors in them, since the wall and carpet will be alike."

"Good idea. One more thing, honey, while we are here, would you go over to the Linens Dept. and pick out a bed bag that you like for both bedrooms?"

"A what ? I don't know what you mean by bed bag."

"Oh, I'm sorry--I guess that is an American product and you probably don't call it that in France. It's a bag that contains two sets of matching sheets and pillow cases, and bedspread with pillow shams, all color coordinated. It sometimes even has extra decorative pillows to go on top of the bedspread."

"Oh how convenient."

"While you are there, pick out a set each of king-size and queen-size down pillows. We may use the bedspread you pick on our bed when we move and put the new one we just bought in the guest room. That is, if you like it better. You can decide later which one you like, so keep it in mind when you are choosing it. I am going to go into the appliance area and look at the large HD television sets while you are doing that. When you are through, come on over and join me and we will decide which one we want for our Den. Okay?"

After they finished their selections, the total came to $25,500. Mr. Wright promised it would all be delivered when they called to say the Condo was ready for occupancy.

When they got home, they had a phone message from Janet, asking them to come over for dinner. Eileen and Keith would also be there so they called back and went over.

Every one was pleased with Renee's progress and with the selections they had made for their furniture. Janet was particularly complimentary to them in getting their thank-you notes written and mailed and for using their time so constructively.

"We will be busy next week getting ready to go to Hawaii for our honeymoon. The Doctor said he would release Renee if everything continued to be good with her. Won't that be wonderful, honey?" he said as he leaned over and gave her a kiss.

"Yes, I am so looking forward to going. I have heard it is really lovely there."

"I will have quite a bit of work to complete at the office before we leave, so I would really appreciate it if one of you Mom, or Eileen, would help Renee prepare for her Permit test. She needs to be ready to get her Permit when we get back so she can start driving lessons."

"I will be glad to do that," Janet said. "Renee, if you want to, why not have Rob drop you off on his way to work and you plan to spend the day or at least the time while he is at the office, with me. I have nothing planned for tomorrow and we can study it together all morning. It won't take you long to be able to pass the test. Then when you feel you are ready, either Eileen or I could take you down to get it."

"Thanks a lot. That is a good idea. I will do it, starting tomorrow."

Eileen looked over at her and smiled. "You can probably learn it in one session but an extra half-day won't hurt you and will give you more confidence when you take the test. I am taking a half day off from the office day after tomorrow for some personal business, which probably will take about an hour. After that, I will come over and study with you the rest of the afternoon."

"That is the day Lois comes to clean. Do you think we might be in her way?"

"That is no problem. I'll just come by and get you and take you to my house and we'll study there."

"That is so nice of both of you. I accept both of your kind offers."

The days continued to pass quickly as Rob had work to do and he and Renee were busily shopping for this and that and making their lists for packing. Renee had spent two half days studying the driving manual and felt she was ready to pass the written test after the session with Eileen. So, as a surprise for Rob, Eileen secretly took her down to take the test, which she passed easily, much to her delight.

When Rob came home that night, Renee had two surprises for him. He was completely amazed that she had made a delicious dinner with pot roast, potatoes and carrots and green beans. She had also made an apple pie.

"Wow, you are really a great cook, honey. Should you be standing up that long at a time to fix a meal? I want to be sure you don't overdo and that you take care of yourself. But this is a scrumptious meal."

"I take it that scrumptious is Texas for good?" said Renee, laughing.

"You bet it is with a capital "S".

"Now, I have another surprise for you. I got my Permit today."

"That is just wonderful news, sweetheart. I am very proud of you, but I am not surprised that you could do it, only that you did it so soon!"

"Thank you for your confidence in me. I just hope I can learn to drive properly and remember the things I should and should not do."

"You will do just fine. Don't worry. When we get back from Hawaii, we will look for a car for you."

"Oh, Rob, do you know yet just when we can go?"

"If the Doctor releases you when we see him tomorrow, we will call the Travel service and see when we can fly to Hawaii and take the ship back. I talked to them this morning and they said that it would be possible to do that," provided we could book passage on the ship within the next three days. We should be able to do that and if everything goes smoothly, we could leave for the Islands in about three or four days. Can you be ready by then?"

"I surely can. In fact, I have been packing my bag with things I want to take for several days now. I have only a little to finish and then I can help you."

The next day, Renee was released and told that she was well enough to travel. She was given instructions to take it easy and not to lift anything heavy. She felt like hugging the Doctor but she just thanked him profusely for all his great care of her. As they walked out of the office, Rob took her in his arms and said, "Let's go pack. We're headed for our honeymoon at last and I am ready!"

"So am I, Darling. I feel like I have been on a long voyage already, waiting for your love for me, and, having found it at last, I want it to keep on and on and on!"

"You have been on a voyage, Honey, and I am with you now on our voyage of life. We are about to take an important side trip, which is to be two wonderful weeks in Hawaii. We are going to cruise and return on the Love Boat. Isn't that romantic?"

"You are always romantic, Sweetheart, and I love you for it. I feel that the journey I took when I started from home was truly my voyage to romance."

"That is true and when you came to me, it was the most important time of my life."

"And also for me. Another was the day we got the letter from you. That was the turning point in my life for sure."

"And mine too. It was really a change in my life when I met you. If only I hadn't been too dumb to realize the real thing at the time."

"Well, at least I grew up in time for you to notice me before you met and married someone else."

The next day, they were all packed and flew to Hawaii. They went First Class and it was fabulous, romantic, and wonderful and neither Rob nor Renee would ever forget what fun they had.

They boarded the Love Boat that afternoon and started their cruise by sailing to all of the islands by night and stopping at each one for the day to sightsee and shop. They made love to each other, bought gifts, took some side trips, had a lot of great food and entertainment. Renee learned to snorkel, and to play Gin Rummy. They played Shuffleboard and swam a lot. They took a lot of pictures for their Honeymoon Scrapbook and had a wonderful time.

They were now ready to get home and start their married life and their new routines. They were full of plans for moving into their new Condo and enjoying all of their new furnishings and wedding gifts.

I am not going to leave you here. Check the Epilogue that follows and find out the rest of the story. It has been great fun introducing you to these two wonderful young people and all of their family and friends.

*　　*　　*

EPILOGUE

SIX MONTHS LATER

Renee parked into the driveway and took her groceries out of the car, and walked to the apartment. She set her bags down and opened the door. She went in, put her bags on the counter and walked out to get the mail from the mail box. She hastily put her perishable items into the refrigerator and sat down to look at the mail. She was very excited to get a letter from her Mom, the first in about two weeks.

Her Mom wrote that she was fine, but that she had been very busy. She had been promoted to Head Nurse at the hospital and had spent several hours training some newly-graduated nurses. She had received a nice raise in salary and had bought herself a much-needed new car. She also wrote that she was very excited that Renee could actually drive now and that she had a car that she really liked.

She said that Ria had been very sick for the last week or so and the Dr. had told them today that she was pregnant. Needless to say, she and Pierre were very pleased. Ria had asked her to tell Renee and to say she would talk with her very soon.

She said that Brandon was coming for a week next month and that she had asked Jim and Janet to come at the same time. She hoped that they would. She said that he had asked her to marry him but she just was not ready to make a commitment. She had just gotten a new job and Ria was there and that they would have a new baby, her first grandchild, to cuddle before long.

She just didn't think she wanted to leave Paris. Renee thought to herself that she was assuming that she would have to leave. "I wonder if Brandon would insist on her moving. Maybe she is just finding an excuse. Hmm-- I do wonder."

She told Renee how proud she was of her taking the classes to become a Paralegal. She was so happy for her that the Condos were going to be ready sooner than they thought. It was exciting that they would be getting to move in before Thanksgiving. Anne said she missed her so much and asked if she could possibly come for a week when Ria's baby was born. Renee was excited at the thought of "going home" to see her Mom and Ria and the new baby. She mentally calculated that she might possibly be able to ask for some time off about that time. Maybe Rob could also take off too so they could both go. She would be a lot happier to go if he went too as she really didn't want to be away from him.

Renee looked at her other mail and sorted it so as to keep the bills all in one place. Rob had been teaching her to do their personal and household bills and she had really been enjoying it. He had said he was very proud of her and she felt a compliment coming from a real Accountant was pretty good. So far, she had not made any major mistakes.

Renee had quite a lot of studying and was learning to use Rob's computer, yet she still had time to cook the meals which she was enjoying a lot. Luckily, they still had Lois to clean, change beds and do the laundry each week so that she could have plenty of time to study, grocery shop, and do the household accounts. Lois was very grateful for the extra work as she was her sole breadwinner and responsible for her own living expenses. They paid her well and she did a wonderful job.

Tomorrow was Saturday and she and Janet were going shopping downtown as there were a lot of sales. She needed some new clothes to wear to school as it was getting close to Fall again. She and Rob were going to a cookout and patio party given by some of their friends tomorrow night.

Mom and Dad Farnsworth had them over to eat some of Maude's wonderful cooking once a week on Thursdays, which they had all agreed on for "Family Night"--a really great idea!

Eileen and Keith were expecting their baby, a girl, according to news they had revealed last week, in two months. There was a shower for Eileen next week. They had picked out "Jamie Lee" for her name. Eileen and Renee had become very close friends so Eileen had shared everything about her pregnancy with her. They had lots of fun shopping for the nursery furniture and clothing then decorating the nursery

In the meantime, Renee and Rob had gotten settled in their new Condo and just loved living there. They were very pleased with their choices of decoration and furniture.

*   *   *

ABOUT NINE MONTHS LATER . . .

Renee flew to Paris to see her Mother and Sister. She had to go alone as she had time off from school, but Rob couldn't take off at the same time. He insisted that she go because she had been lonesome to see them. She only had a week, but she hated to be away from Rob even that long. It was really worth it, however, to see her family and to get to hold little Angela Anne in her arms. Even though she didn't get to come when she was born, she decided that because she was a little older, it was more satisfying to see her smile and giggle out loud. She was adorable and Renee started feeling like she was ready to have one too.

Jim and Janet had not been able to make the trip earlier, but planned to early next year in the Spring. They hoped to be there when Brandon came. Anne was still in close touch with Brandon as they wrote letters and talked by phone often.

When Renee returned home, she had only three months left to finish her Paralegal course and then she wanted to start looking for a job. Rob repeated that she did not have to work but he could understand her wanting to put her newly-acquired skills in practice, and encouraged her in whatever she wanted to do.

*   *   *

ONE YEAR LATER

Renee and Rob were both enjoying their new niece, Jamie, and frequently offered to baby sit. They said they were getting in practice for themselves for later.

Renee had been working for six months for a small legal firm with three partners and was completely enthralled with the work she was learning to do. She loved making good money for the first time in her life. Since she was working, they had decided to keep Lois on full time and have her do the evening meal on weekdays, except Thursdays, which continued to be Family Night. On weekends, she and Rob loved cooking together. If they didn't want to cook, they went out to a nice restaurant.

Since Renee had been working and using her car a lot more and Rob's car had a lot of miles on it by now, they decided to splurge and buy each of them a new Lexus. Meantime Jim and Janet took their trip to Paris to see Anne for a couple of weeks and were joined there by Brandon. Anne took some vacation and they traveled by car throughout Europe for a marvelous trip.

Ria and Pierre and little Angela were coming to the States for a visit and Renee was so excited. They decided to rent a crib for Angela and bought her a few new toys. They would be here only for a week so there would be very little time for sight seeing.

Rob's business had grown by leaps and bounds and he had added two new CPAs, an administrative assistant and two computer operators. He said if the business grew any more, he would have to have a larger building as the current office space was filled to capacity.

Rob and Renee began to talk more about starting a family, but decided to buy a house before having a baby. There was a new development being built near the Country Club and Golf

Course and they looked at lots there. One of the models there was a two-story Georgian style home and they immediately fell in love with it.

It had five bedrooms, three full baths and a powder room downstairs. It had a large living room with a fireplace of white brick, a large dining room and a huge country kitchen. It also had a den and a laundry room. It also boasted a sitting room upstairs near the Master bedroom. It was decorated with furniture almost identical to theirs so they could envision moving right into it. There was also a covered patio and an in-ground kidney-shaped pool with a hot tub nearby. They decided on that model and bought a beautiful big lot with shade trees in front. They selected a location one street over from the golf course so that they would not be bothered with stray golf balls and window breakage, certain to become a problem on the lots next to the Course.

They picked up the brochures and took them home to select their wallpaper, flooring, carpeting, paint and tile. They were told it would be at least a year before they would be able to start building it as they had so many more homes to be built which were ordered ahead of them. It would take about three to six months to build, depending on weather and unforeseen problems since they would be building several in the area at once. They talked to the Lessor of the Condos and he said he would forgive the few months remaining on their new two-year lease if there was some when they were able to move to their house. Consequently, they renewed their lease on the Condo for two more years.

A few weeks later, Renee woke up morning very sick and Rob took her to the Doctor, who told her, after taking a few tests, that she was, as she had begun to suspect, pregnant. The plans people make don't always work out as anticipated! But even though they had planned for this to happen later, they were very happy about it and couldn't wait to tell their parents.

They immediately started mentally decorating the little sitting room for a nursery in the new house and got so excited they started clearing out the den in the Condo for a nursery there, making room for the baby furniture they would go and buy. Eileen, of course, was delighted to help her select furniture and decorate the nursery as Renee had done for her.

Her friends gave her a baby shower and she got a lot of lovely gifts. She had become friends with a lot of Eileen's friends, had also met some lovely people at Church with whom she had become close, especially Lynn Thornton. She had met a couple of girls who worked in her office that she liked a lot too so she felt that she had become a real Texan by now.

So nine months later, William James Farnsworth a beautiful baby boy, named for both Grandfathers, made his appearance. They planned to call him Bill. All grandparents were absolutely pleased as punch.

Renee had worked up through her seventh month as she felt fine. She was completely thrilled about her new role as Mother and was, of course, very busy with little Bill and treasured every minute of it. She was also enjoying cooking new things in her own kitchen.

She kept in touch with her friends she had made at work and while she wouldn't exchange her current job for it, she missed the work she had learned to do, because it had been so interesting to her. Rob was also very pleased over being a father and spent as much time as possible with the baby when he was home.

Rob and Renee had become involved in a "42 Club" which is a game any Texan would know about. There were eight couples from church who liked to play and met on Friday nights alternating at a different house each week. For those of who don't know about 42, it is a domino game, similar to the card game of bridge and a little like pinochle.

Eileen and Keith's little girl was a year old now and it was fun for Renee and Rob to watch her grow. They were very fond of her and still managed to baby sit her when possible. Jamie was fascinated with her new cousin.

Renee had just talked with her Mother and Ria to tell them all about her new baby boy. She had promised to give an update often to Anne who was very anxious to see her new grandson. Anne said she was coming over just as soon as she could arrange to be off work for a couple of weeks. She thought she would be able to get a replacement on board this week and would have everything packed to leave as soon as possible.

It is hard to leave all of these nice people, but it is necessary to end their story on a very happy note. That, of course, is the whole point of the story--a feel-good read! There may be another one coming to see what happens to the lives of some of the other characters. I wouldn't be surprised So long for now.

*   *   *

With Best Wishes
Jeanne